# THE QUARTERBACK AND THE GHOST

# THE QUARTERBACK AND THE GHOST

## J.R. MORNINGSTAR

iUniverse, Inc.
New York   Bloomington

iUniverse books may be ordered through booksellers or by contacting:

iUniverse
1663 Liberty Drive
Bloomington, IN 47403
www.iuniverse.com
1-800-Authors (1-800-288-4677)

Because of the dynamic nature of the Internet, any Web addresses or links contained in this book may have changed since publication and may no longer be valid. The views expressed in this work are solely those of the author and do not necessarily reflect the views of the publisher, and the publisher hereby disclaims any responsibility for them.

ISBN: 978-1-4502-6147-0 (sc)
ISBN: 978-1-4502-6153-1 (ebook)

Printed in the United States of America

iUniverse rev. date: 09/30/2010

Dedicated to the enduring spirit of Larry Morningstar
"Long May You Run"

▼

## CHAPTER ONE

**OCTOBER 1988**

This was no time to panic. The football was on the Saint Thomas twenty-four yard line. The quarterback Gallegan called out the signals. "Blue thirty-two…blue thirty-two…" Gallegan took the snap and drifted back to pass. Mike Brown was open in the flat; he caught a wobbly pass and scampered to the fifteen before crashing to the turf after a hard tackle. A quick opener with the fullback got the first down. One of the referees was looking intently at his watch.

Coach Mike sent in the next play with a flanker sub. There was time for maybe two more plays. The football was hiked. Gallegan couldn't get a handle on it! The ball tumbled to the turf and rolled over end over end, but the center pounced on it, a five-yard loss.

Ten seconds were left. One more play. Gallegan accepted the snap from the center and sprinted out to the right—side-stepped an onrushing tackler—looked for anyone open—faked out a linebacker—took off for the end zone. The ten…the five…two defenders at the goal line—Gallegan leaped between them, all three came down in a heap—the referee threw his hands in the air. Touchdown!

Our Lady of Perpetual Health won by two; there was no need to kick the extra point. The team charged out to mob Gallegan. This win put Our Lady in first place in the Blue division of the South Bend Inner City Catholic League. Coach Mike patted Gallegan on the back and pulled off the helmet. Gallegan's long strawberry blond hair, once held up by bobby pins, fell to her shoulders. That's right, Gallegan, Mary Alice Gallegan, was a girl, and she was the star quarterback for the Our Lady Panthers.

Mary Alice freed herself from the hugs of her teammates. Except for one. "I could have gotten us that touchdown," Todd Hertel hissed. He gave Mary Alice a shove before moving away. Todd was the starting quarterback last season. That little fact did not matter a bit to Coach Mike Zersky. With his big shoulders and crooked nose that had obviously been broken, maybe in a fight, Coach Mike was not one to argue with. He was new this season, and since he had no knowledge of the previous year, he started whoever showed the most promise in practice, and that was Mary Alice. Even though it was her first time out for the football team, and even though she had the audacity to be a girl, she still beat out Todd for the starting position. Todd's dad was an All-American quarterback at Purdue. For Todd and his dad, being replaced by a girl, or anyone, was unacceptable. After all, Purdue will need a top-notch signal caller in a few years and father and son Hertel planned on Todd being that quarterback. No prissy Barbie Doll quarterback was going to get in their way.

Mary Alice scanned the sidelines, looking for her dad, Chuck Gallegan. He promised to be at the game. There he was, talking to two men. One of the men handed her dad something green; it had to be money. Mary Alice's shook her head in disgust.

"Kitten, nice game," Chuck yelled at his daughter, quickly shoving the money in his back pocket. Kitten! Mary Alice hated being called that name, especially in front of people she didn't know. She's thirteen years old. You don't call a teenage girl Kitten in 1988, maybe in the fifties, not in the eighties.

"Dad, I saw you put that money in your pocket...you gambled on this game, didn't you."

"Kitten, the man owed me some money...."

"Don't lie to me Dad."

Mary Alice turned to walk away, her face a crimson red. Chuck, tall and a little over weight with a turned up nose, planted himself in front of her. "C'mon Kitten, with you playing quarterback, it's a sure thing," he said. "This isn't gambling...its taking money given freely to me by some real dumb guys."

Chuck snatched the dough out of his pocket and held it up. "Look, a hundred bucks, it would take me three days work to make that kind of money."

"But you promised not to gamble anymore" Mary Alice whined." She broke into a trot. "I'll see you at home," she said back to her dad.

"Hey, don't you want a ride?" Chuck shouted. Mary Alice ignored him. Her sad blue eyes blinked back tears.

Gambling! Mary Alice had learned to hate that word. It's a sickness, the head doctor told her at the clinic. It can destroy lives. It can definitely destroy families. Mary Alice knew this only too well.

Becky Gallegan left home last year. Mary Alice's mom. Couldn't put up with it anymore. She couldn't put up with paychecks lost to card games. She worked two jobs trying to make ends meet. It still was not enough. When loans could not be repaid, Becky insisted Chuck get some help with his compulsive gambling. He fought it at first, but when she threatened to leave him, he agreed to see the psychiatrists at the clinic. And it helped for a while. But then he went on a gambling binge, lost the Christmas money, ruining another holiday. Becky left on New Year's Eve. Mary Alice would pick up the ringing telephone two or three two times a week since then and no one would talk on the other end of the line. When the phone rang, she knew somehow, that it was her mother. She would picture her standing there, the phone pressed to her ear, a slim woman, with dark brown hair that hung to her shoulders. Her mother used to laugh with a hiccup, and that would make her laugh all the more. But now there was nothing but a silent line. Mary Alice knew it was her. She could feel her through the phone, and that made her love her mother more than ever. "Please come home, I miss you so much," she would tell her mother, but there would be no answer, and her mother would hang up.

The sun was setting fast as Mary Alice, bone tired, trudged into Cook's Woods. This twisted cluster of mostly dead trees, the property of mean old Mrs. Cook, was a shortcut to Mary Alice's house. Something was just not right about these woods. Shadows loomed everywhere. Was it a haunted forest? Did ghosts appear among the dead trees? That was what most of the kids at school thought.

Mary Alice pulled up, not sure of how she felt. Might not be such a good idea to go through these woods. The wind was gusting, pushing the scraggy tree branches against her face. She turned around in a circle, which caused her to fall against a slimy moss covered stump. Good thing she was still wearing her shoulder pads.

It was getting dark. Presently there was a soft moan, a whisper in the wind. "We are watching you…we are watching you" the moaning seemed to be saying. Mary Alice got up off her knees and looked around. Were the trees talking to her? That's ridiculous. Trees can't talk. And it can't be ghosts. There are no such things as ghosts.

Still, she began to move at a quicker pace through the woods, not stopping before coming to the clearing that fronted her house. Chuck's old beat-up pickup truck was not in the gravel driveway. He probably stopped at Smithy's poolroom. After all, he had extra cash in his pocket. There are a lot of sheep to fleece at Smithy's, he always tells Mary Alice. Thinks he's a great pool shark. How come he always came home with empty pockets?

The house seemed so empty and cold without her mother being there. Sighing, Mary Alice went to her bedroom and removed her sweat-stained football jersey. She looked at herself in the vanity mirror above her dresser drawers. Her face was streaked with dirt, and black eye shadow ran down her cheeks. She looked scary, sort of like a football playing vampire. The spooky moaning from the woods was still on her mind. Was it a warning? "There are no such things as ghosts," she said out loud, as if to reassure herself one more time. "And trees can't talk." But she could not shake the feeling that several great big eyeballs had her in their sights.

## Chapter Two

The night was still except for the occasional fluttering of a bat passing by or the hoot of an owl searching for food. The wind continued to whistle through Cook's Woods, scuttling crispy leaves about in the draft. Threatening clouds, not there a minute ago, began to thicken. And that is when several long black creatures flew out of the woods. They were flying serpents.

The serpents rose into the night sky, searching about with eyes wide and red. Muffled cries came out of their tightly clenched jaws of bone. They darted over the field a few minutes before hovering over Mary Alice's cinder block house. Just then her dad steered his truck around the oak tree at the top of the driveway, shuddering to a stop by the side door porch.

Chuck Gallegan staggered out of the pickup and immediately glanced up, to the top of the slant tile roof. He thought something was flying over his head, but he couldn't see anything to be sure, too dark, he guessed. That dang overnight streetlight was burnt out again. When he put his house key into the door lock, he heard a low wail, like that of a frightened child, and he thought of Mary Alice. Chuck hurried down the front hall, and after coming to a sudden stop, he quietly opened the door to Mary Alice's bedroom, hoping she was not the source of the sorrowful moan. She seemed to be fine, sound to sleep, the quilt that once belonged to her mother pulled up to her sweet face. It must have been the wind going through the eaves. And with that belief in mind, Chuck retired to his bed.

The wind began to blow harder. The flying serpents, fueled by the windblasts, were not ready to find a place to rest. They continued to fly in circles until one of the serpents streaked down the house's red brick chimney, coming out of the sooty fireplace. The serpent was inside the house.

The serpent went through the living room wall like it wasn't there, moving down the hall, taking its time. The house seemed to hold its breath. Grandfather's old clock, standing sentry in the hallway, struck twelve. Midnight—the witching hour! The serpent lingered just outside Chuck's closed bedroom door. It seemed to be listening—and it listened some more before going through the door, at first levitating over a dresser, then over a chair that was draped by a pair of blue jeans, and then over the bed that cradled Chuck. Coming closer, the serpent came within an inch of Chuck's face.

Coughing, sputtering, Chuck woke up with a jolt. The hair on the back of his neck bristled. Sitting up, looking around, Chuck squinted into the darkness. Big black shadows danced across the bedroom wall, sent from the headlights of a passing car. Cool wind blew in through the open bedroom window. Chuck suddenly felt very cold. He slowly eased out of his bed, being very careful not to trip as he stepped across the creaking hardwood floor. It did not take him very long to slam the bedroom window shut. Then Chuck was back in his bed, yanking the covers tight. He soon fell into a fitful sleep.

The serpent was hiding on the ceiling, invisible in the dark. It made its way to the wall, and was through it, back in the hallway, searching for Mary Alice.

She couldn't wake up. Her arms flailed about wildly, trying to fight back the bad dream. It didn't seem to matter; the nightmare could not be stopped. Pink sky turned into dark clouds. Lightning flashed but there was no thunder. A beautiful woman, her mother, held out her arms as if to give her a big hug, but she dissolved into dust, and was gone. Then Mary Alice was running in Cook's Woods, with demon dogs chasing her, their sharp fangs ripping at her legs, and she couldn't get away. She stumbled over a big rock, the dogs upon her, everything spinning around...

Mary Alice opened her eyes, fully awake, letting out her breath so hard it made her throat hurt. She sat up quickly, and peered at the bright dials on her alarm clock. Several more hours until morning! Sleep would not come easy the rest of this night. She laid back in her bed, her ears roaring and her heart pounding. Shivers ran down her spine. Her bedroom had turned into a fuzzy world of fear.

The black flying serpent hunkered down beneath Mary Alice's bed, and waited for the dawn.

# CHAPTER THREE

▼

When Mary Alice woke up from a fitful sleep, grey October light was filtering in through her bedroom window. Far away, the sad, lonely whistle of the New York Central train broke through the early morning quiet. Then her alarm clock made that hideous sound all alarm clocks make. Time to get up.

Mary Alice sat up and groaned with the pain in her head. Too little sleep. It might have been better to stay up all night. She finally pushed herself out of bed. Before heading for the bathroom, she felt around for her slippers. All her bare feet could feel was the cold floor. The slippers were not where they should be, at the foot of her bed. She searched around the room, but then thought, oh, they must be under the bed. Stiff muscles from the previous day's game made it hard for her to get down on her knees. The quilt had fallen to the side of the bed, hiding what was underneath. Mary Alice stretched out a hand—and pulled back the quilt. No slippers. Just dust balls.

Yawning, stretching, Mary Alice got back on her feet. Ah, the heck with the slippers. After brushing her teeth and taking a hot shower to get the cobwebs out, she went to the kitchen to get breakfast ready for herself and her dad. He came in right after Mary Alice poured the milk over the Cheerios.

"Mornin' Kitten," Chuck told her as he sat down at the kitchen table. "I was watching you yesterday at the game. You gotta be a little higher with your passes. Remember what I've been telling you, throw into the receivers hands."

Mary Alice turned her back and rolled her eyes. Chuck was a first team all conference quarterback in high school and thought he knew all there was to know about football.

"How did it go at the pool hall last night," Mary Alice asked as she joined her dad at the table.

"Oh, I just play for laughs," he said between spoonfuls of Cheerios. "Pass the sugar, will ya." Chuck always poured mountains of sugar on his cereal.

"How much money did you lose?" Mary Alice squirmed in her chair knowing what the answer would be.

"Not much, Kitten. You gotta put some money down to make it interesting."

That means he probably lost a couple hundred. Mary Alice had heard this before. Same old tune.

Sometimes she thought she hated him.

"Gotta go to school," she cried out, her voice louder that she wanted it to be.

"All right Kitten," Chuck said calmly. "You don't have to broadcast it over the whole neighborhood."

Mary Alice wanted her dad to throw his arms around her so she could curl up in a little ball and feel warm and secure. Instead he belched and shoved himself away from the table.

"I got you the job selling programs at the game tomorrow," Chuck called over his shoulder as left the kitchen.

Her dad worked as a maintenance man at the University of Notre Dame. He did all kinds of odd jobs, whatever was needed, from mopping floors to setting up chairs. On football Saturdays, he helped the stadium grounds crew with the field tarp, and for doing this, he got two free hot dogs and free admission to the game. Chuck knew the man who was in charge of selling game day programs. Somebody he gambled with, naturally. It took all his power of persuasion to convince the man that Mary Alice could sell programs as well as any boy. After all, she was her team's quarterback.

Regardless, Mary Alice was glad to have a chance to earn a little spending money.

Mary Alice slipped on her nylon jacket, grabbed her books and an over ripe banana off the kitchen table, and made a getaway from the house. She just didn't feel comfortable at home anymore. Chuck was in his own little gambling world, and Mary Alice did not want to live there—no way. So sometimes it just felt good to have somewhere else to go, anyplace, even if it was school.

Ricardo was not sitting on the porch swing, his usual spot, when Mary Alice stopped in front of the white picket fence that bordered his house. Mary Alice walked Ricardo to school almost every day. She had just opened the squeaky fence gate when Ricardo's mother, a plump faced woman, came out to meet her. "Ricardo's running a little late today, Mary Alice," she said, almost singing the words. "He'll be out in a couple of minutes."

"That's okay, Mrs. Amigo, I'll wait for him right here," Mary Alice said politely.

"You are such a good friend to Ricardo, si, es verdad," Mrs. Amigo told her as she dabbed an eye with a corner of the multi-colored flowered apron she was wearing. She went back into the house.

Something bad happened to Ricardo when he was ten. He had an accident with his skateboard. Wasn't watching where he was going, so he ran his skateboard into a parked car. He hurt his head pretty bad. It was two months before he came out of a coma. That was not the end of his misery. Three operations followed in the next two years. A metal plate was put in his head. The doctors did all they could, but Ricardo still had trouble with his speech—he talked slowly and carefully, like he had to think of each word before he could say it.

"Good...morning," Ricardo hollered as he ran through the open gate.

"Hi Ricardo, here's your banana," Mary Alice said, handing him the fruit. She would bring him a banana every day. Didn't know why or how it started, it was just something she did.

"Thank...you... Mary...Alice."

Ricardo peeled back the banana and plopped half of it in his mouth. Then before Mary Alice knew what he was up to, Ricardo started down the street at a fast clip. Mary Alice unfortunately knew where he was headed. They stopped in front of a construction site, where a new house was being built, and there it was, a Caterpillar tractor, the kind that pushes dirt around. Ricardo loved construction equipment.

"Ricardo, don't climb onto that tractor," Mary Alice shouted, but it was too late, Ricardo was already sitting on the driver's seat. Mary Alice plopped down next to him. "We're gonna get another late slip," she told him sternly. "I don't want to have to stay after school."

"Oh…okay…Mary…Alice," Ricardo said, sounding disappointed.

Mary Alice thought for a bit. "Oh, stay where you are," she said with a wink. "The workers won't be here for a while yet. We've got a few minutes."

That brought a big smile to Ricardo's face. He grabbed the stirring wheel, pretending to drive while making big truck noises. Mary Alice joined in, and the two of them made a sizable whirling sound. The sun played peek-a-boo through the thick morning clouds, splashing the surrounding work site with vacant dark spots. The boy and the girl felt good, even happy.

Mary Alice sighed heavily. "You know, we really do have to get to school."

"I…know," Ricardo said, resigned to their fate.

They began their descent, holding on carefully to the tractor before jumping onto a dirt pile. Whoosh! Something darted from the top of the Cat, nipping Mary Alice's right arm. Something black.

"Did you see that?" Mary Alice screamed.

"See…what?" Ricardo looked around wildly, ducking his head.

For a moment, Mary Alice was light-headed. She clung to the side of the tractor to keep her balance.

"Are...you...all... right?" Ricardo asked. He started to tremble a bit.

Mary Alice breathed in deeply but was able to manage a hint of a grin. She rolled up her sleeve and rubbed her arm. There was no mark. "I think so," she said slowly. "Just a dizzy spell, I guess."

Without saying another word, they were on their way to school. Their reflections raced ahead of them on the sidewalk—black shadows. Mary Alice walked a little faster. For once, she couldn't wait to be seated at her desk for her first hour class.

## Chapter Four

▼

The morning clouds were turning stormy as Mary Alice and Ricardo approached the school. "Please don't let us be late again," Mary Alice begged God silently as they ran across the school playground. Ricardo was lagging behind.

"Hurry Ricardo, the bell is gonna ring."

"I'm…hurrying…Mary…Alice."

The bell rang. Dang! Late for the third time this month. They would have to stay after school for sure.

Sister Barbara Ann was seeing red as Mary Alice and Ricardo took their seats. Maybe if they scrunched down, their desks would hide them. Fat chance!

"Ricardo… Mary Alice… would you present yourselves at my desk immediately please," Sister told them icily.

Mary Alice bit her lower lip and exhaled. To avoid meeting Sister's angry gaze, she slowly trudged forward with her eyes studying her shoes, joining an equally slow moving Ricardo at Sister's desk. Behind them, the rest of the class was sniggering with their hands clasped over their mouths.

"Class…get out your history books and start reading chapter four," Sister said, peering over Ricardo's shoulder. "And I don't want to hear a peep from anyone."

Rain pelted the window next to the desk. A flash of lightning lit Sister's face, giving her an even more severe appearance. "Look at me, Mary Alice," she said sharply. "Do you have any excuses for constantly being late?"

"No sister."

"And do you have any excuses, Ricardo?"

"…No," he said meekly.

"My, my," Sister said, "it seems I won't have to ask for volunteers to clasp erasures after school today. Now go back to your desks and start reading your history assignment."

"Yes Sister," Mary Alice and Ricardo said at the same time.

The sniggering began again as Mary Alice and Ricardo returned to their desks. Especially from Todd Hertel. He really enjoyed trouble coming Mary Alice's way. But the other kids seemed to enjoy it too. The girls considered Mary Alice a turncoat—not one of them. Who did she think she was—Super Girl? She runs like a guy, tackles like a guy, and throws a football like a guy. If a spectator saw her in football gear, that person would swear she was a guy. Girls were cheerleaders. Maybe they played softball or volleyball. Nothing more. And the boys in the class? Well, they were just plain jealous that a girl could play football better than they could.

Tears welled up in Mary Alice's eyes. Except for Ricardo, it seemed that she no longer had any friends.

She looked out the classroom window at the windblown rain. No doubt about it, she would have trouble keeping her mind on her studies.

The rest of the morning passed by at a snail's pace. Lunch period came none too soon.

The school cafeteria was a bustle of activity with kids coming in, grabbing trays, and getting in line to purchase the special beans and weenies dinner. A low hum filled the room, a chattering of rising young voices all talking at once. Most of the eighth graders sat together at the main table. Mary Alice sat down with Ricardo at a table away from the other kids. She just didn't feel like being next to anyone right now, except for Ricardo.

"Hey, how's it going," a tall thin girl with curly brown hair said, stopping at Mary Alice's side.

"Oh…Hi Louise…ah…do you want to sit with us?" Mary Alice motioned to an empty chair next to Ricardo.

Louise smiled. "I'm going over to the table with the other girls. Thanks anyway." She started moving away but suddenly stopped. "Hey Mary Alice," she said curtly. "Sorry you can't make it to my slumber party tonight."

Mary Alice just stared at her. "You didn't invite me."

"Yea, well, I really wanted to, but the other girls said they wouldn't come if you did." Louise's eyes narrowed. "You know, if you would give up that football garbage, I think the other girls would accept you better."

Mary Alice looked at Louise, and then at the other girls, and then at Louise again. "I can't give up football, I love it too much."

But where was football going to take her. Mary Alice wouldn't be allowed to play in high school; she knew that. How could she love something that made her so unpopular?

"See you around," Mary Alice said, turning away.

Louise looked surprised. "Yea, see ya." She walked over to the eighth grade table to sit with the other girls. Mary Alice watched her out of the corners of her eyes. Louise had always been her best friend, ever since they first started kindergarten. Since the end of summer, though, they seemed to be going in different directions.

Why did it have to be that way?

"Well, if it isn't Wonder Woman and her faithful sidekick Retardo."

It was Todd Hertel and his moronic friends David and Mathew. They were standing there with their arms crossed trying to look like real tough guys. It wasn't working.

"Get lost Todd," Mary Alice said. Her voice was as cold as the North Pole.

Todd leaned toward her, just waiting for her to say something else.

"Yea…get…lost…Todd, "said Ricardo, puffing up his chest.

"Oh, Retardo can talk. Look it that boys, it can talk," Todd said with a snicker. The two other boys laughed like this was the funniest joke they had ever heard.

Mary Alice made a motion to get up. "If you're going to insult Ricardo, you will have to answer to me."

"I…can…take…care…of…myself… Mary Alice," but before Ricardo could say another word, Todd slung an arm around his shoulder and squeezed hard enough to crack bones.

"You can take a joke, can't you, Retardo,"

Ricardo began to sputter and choke, so Todd released him. Sister Rose Marie, the lunch hour monitor, was standing in the cafeteria doorway, frowning at the entire scene.

"What seems to be the problem here?" Sister asked sternly.

"Good afternoon, Sister," Todd said as if he was the best boy scout ever. "We just stopped by to say hello. I was showing Ricardo how to make a tackle. Well, we better get going to our next class."

The boys hurried out of the cafeteria.

"If those boys are bothering you two," said Sister Rose Marie, "let me know."

Mary Alice let out another big sigh. "That won't be necessary, Sister. Thanks anyway."

Sister opened her mouth as if to say something more, but she just shrugged and walked away.

Somehow, the afternoon rolled into afterschool. The rain had stopped before the final bell. Mary Alice and Ricardo were outside clapping erasers, their penance for being late for school. Chalk dust was swirling about, plugging up their nostrils and causing their eyes to water. They had to stop every few minutes to blow their noses. Ricardo eventually reached into a back pocket of his dress jeans and pulled out a red and white bandana that he securely tied over his mouth and nose. No such luck for Mary Alice. All she had was a couple of Kleenex.

Finally, after a few more claps, the job was done. Mary Alice and Ricardo gathered the erasers in a laundry basket and took them back to the empty classroom.

A voice rang out. "Let me see how good a job you did." The children spun around and found themselves looking at Sister Barbara Ann. She peered into the basket. "Looks like you two did a very good job. You can go home now."

Mary Alice and Ricardo were heading for the cloakroom to grab their jackets when Sister abruptly said, "Ricardo, would you wait out in the hall for a few minutes. I would like to have a word with Mary Alice in private."

"Sure…Sister." Ricardo retrieved his jacket and left the classroom, closing the door behind him.

"Pull up a chair, Mary Alice," Sister said, her tone softer. "This won't take long."

Mary Alice was nervous. What did she do wrong now?

"You're not in any kind of trouble, so relax," Sister told her. "I just want to know how your home life is going. Has your mother returned home?"

"No–she… hasn't," Mary Alice said under her breath. She fidgeted in her chair. "How…how do you know about my mother?"

"I always make it my business to know as much as possible about my students."

"Then…then you know about my father!" Mary Alice buried her face in her hands. She began to quietly sob.

Sister Barbara Ann placed a soft hand on her quivering shoulder. "It's okay to cry, Mary Alice. It will make you feel better."

Mary Alice raised her head and looked directly into Sister's limpid green eyes. Maybe Sister was someone to trust, someone she could talk to about how she really feels.

"Yes, I know about your father's gambling habits," Sister said. "I do some counseling in the parish rectory, and he has talked to me about it."

Sister didn't say anything for a little while, and then said at last, "My brother was a heavy gambler. The one thing I have learned is that a gambler will not quit until he admits he has a problem. And I'm sorry to say your dad is not ready to confess anything is wrong."

Mary Alice's mind was clouded. She had to think hard about what Sister was telling her. "I want him to stop gambling," she said harshly. "It's so horrible what it has done to my family."

"I know just how you're feeling," Sister said. "All you can do right now is love and support him. Don't give up hope."

"Yes Sister."

Sister Barbara Ann rose and gave Mary Alice a look of grave concern. "Now go home and get some rest. Try to forget your problems for a while."

Before Mary Alice opened the classroom door, she asked Sister, "What happened to your brother? Did he ever get over his gambling?"

Sister's eyes turned sad. "No, I'm afraid not. I haven't seen him in ten years."

Mary Alice was gasping as she joined Ricardo in the hallway. "Let's go home," she said wistfully. They left the school, going back over the playground. In a matter of minutes they were in front of Ricardo's house.

"See...you...Monday," Ricardo said to Mary Alice as he opened the fence gate.

"Have a good weekend, Ricardo."

Ricardo scooted into his house. Mary Alice continued walking, alone, which was just fine with her. She needed to do some pretty serious thinking. Sister's words were swirling through her brain. How could she love and support her dad and yet find a way to end his compulsive gambling? She was mad—and also afraid. Her fear was the main thing. Fear made her feel she was not in charge of her life. Mom was gone. Would dad soon follow her out the door? Then what would happen to her? Maybe that was why she played football—as a quarterback she was in complete control of the offense, and she liked that feeling of being in complete control.

But it all came down to this—she wanted a normal family life again.

She was becoming aware that a car was following her closely. She would stop, and the car would stop. It was a big black car, maybe a Caddy or a Chrysler. Turning around in small circles, she continued to check on the car. She was starting to sweat.

The car pulled up to the curb. A man a man rolled down the passenger side window, a creepy looking man with a face like a ferret. "Tell your dad if he knows what's good for him, he will pay up his gambling debts," the man snarled. The car then sped off around the next street corner and was out of sight.

Mary Alice stood still in the middle of the sidewalk. She licked her lips and tasted salt. Trembling, her stomach turned to ice. There was only one thought on her mind as she started to run. Had to get home fast and warn her dad!

▼

## CHAPTER FIVE

"Did you hear what I said, Dad? Those men want their money!"

Mary Alice lay under the covers, thinking about her conversation with her dad the previous night, wondering why her Dad was so unconcerned. She told him what had happened on her way home from school but he didn't seem to care. In fact, he just laughed. "Those guys are friends of mine trying to be funny," he told her. "Nothing to worry about."

But she wasn't so sure.

It was Saturday morning, a chance to sleep-in. She could sleep forever. Wait a minute! Forgetting her weariness, she sat up and shoved back the covers. This time she really wanted to get out of bed. Today was the day she was going to hawk programs at the Notre Dame, Stanford game. It would be her very first time inside Notre Dame Stadium, and she was very excited about it. She'd have a chance to see her favorite player, Tony Rice, play quarterback for the undefeated Fighting Irish. Maybe he would run for a couple of touchdowns. A win today would be a giant step in Notre Dame's quest for the 1988 National Championship, and that would be all right with her.

Later in the morning, Mary Alice rode with her dad to the campus maintenance building. There was nothing to say to each other, so they just listened to music on the truck radio. Once there, Chuck Gallegan punched the time clock, and then he and Mary Alice began walking across the campus to the stadium. The enticing smells of roasted hot dogs, hamburgers, and bratwursts greeted their nostrils, coming from the grills of the tailgaters that were spread throughout the campus quads. Small boys were throwing footballs to each other, dreaming of the day they would put on the blue and gold uniform of the Fighting Irish. On the steps of the Administration Building, the Marching Band was giving a sizable crowd an early halftime show. It was a sunny day, but cool and crisp. A perfect October football Saturday.

They finally approached the red brick stadium, with Chuck going through the main gate to report for his ground crew duties. Mary Alice went around the stadium until she found gate 11. That was where the boss of the program sellers was located. He was a stooped man crammed inside a rumpled suit a size too small. His hair was bald in spots while his face was long and thin, and he wore black horn-rimmed glasses. His name was Mr. Lackey.

"Now fellas," he said with a squeaky voice to the kids gathered around him, "grab a box of programs and follow me…okie dokie?

Mary Alice snatched a box of programs that were stacked against a wall and went with everyone else directly outside gate 11. They were all boys, except for her.

Mr. Lackey fixed his beady eyes on the boys—and Mary Alice. "Now fellas," he continued speaking, "take your box of programs and go around to the parking lots and tailgate parties or wherever you see people and sell them a program...okie dokie?" He bent over stiffly and picked one up, waving it over his head. "Fellas, here's how you do it. You yell—programs—get your programs—four dollars—get your programs...okie dokie?"

It was all Mary Alice could do to keep from laughing out loud. Mr. Mackey was hilariously hopping about, thrusting the program wildly in the air, yelling "get your programs!" She wisely just eked out a smile.

"Okay fellas, let's go out and sell...okie dokie?" Mr. Lackey told everyone. "And keep this in your mind," he added, "don't even think about pocketing any of the money—I keep a strict inventory on everything and I will know if you are stealing...okie dokie?"

Mr. Lackey turned around to go back inside gate 11, but he saw Mary Alice and stopped dead on his tracks. He motioned her over. "Now young lady," he said, "I normally don't let girls sell programs, but I told your dad I would allow it just this one time, as a favor, and also because I owe him money I lost at poker, so do a good job and don't let me down...okie dokie?"

Mary Alice nodded. "I get to go inside and sell program once the game starts—right?" She asked sweetly.

Mr. Lackey cleared his throat loudly. "Yes, see me here at gate 11 when the game starts and I will set you up to sell inside...okie dokie?'

"Okie dokie," Mary Alice repeated. She grabbed her box of programs and headed out to hawk them. But the whole time she was thinking "the only way I got this job was because Mr. Lackey owed my dad money." More and more it seemed gambling ruled her life.

This was easier than she thought it would be. Mary Alice took her programs directly to where the buses were bringing in out of town fans. All she had to do was stand in a one spot and wait for the fans to get off the buses. Practically all of them bought a program. She went back and got two more boxes. Selling the programs was a breeze.

Todd Hertel and one of his dopey friends were hanging around the busses, asking people if they had any extra tickets. "How about giving us a free program," Todd told her with a slightly wicked grin. Before she could give him an emphatic no, he reached into a box, but Mary Alice was too quick for him, and she grabbed his arm. She squeezed his arm tightly.

"Oww, let go, I was only teasing," Todd hollered. Then he began to giggle. "Don't get so riled up, Mary Alice."

She let go of Todd's arm. Immediately the boys hightailed out of there, mixing in with the other football devotees.

Good riddance, she thought. And then she forgot all about the boys because the game was about to start.

Gate 11 was very crowded when Mary Alice approached. The last minute fans were streaming in, so Mary Alice pressed against them, forcing herself to the front of the ticket turnstile.

The ticket taker asked her for a game ticket, but Mr. Lackey came up and told him she was going to sell programs.

"Alright, go about your business," the ticket taker said, waving Mary Alice inside.

"Fella…er, lady," Mr. Lackey said, "go get some more programs. Then I want you to go up and down the aisles and yell out you have programs to sell…okie dokie? Mr. Lackey began hopping around again with a program high in the air. This time Mary Alice couldn't stifle a chuckle. No matter, Mr. Lackey didn't seem to notice, he just kept on talking. "Now I don't want to catch you sitting down on an empty seat watching the game…okie dokie? I will be watching you."

Mary Alice eagerly grabbed another box of programs. Just ahead of her was the portal to the playing field. She stood there for a second or two, and then stepped outside.

The Notre Dame marching band was spread out on the emerald green turf formed in a giant ND, playing the national anthem, so Mary Alice got to pause and drink in the scene. All the spectators in the stands were on their feet, the men with their caps over their hearts. Down below, the kilt-attired Irish Guard was raising the stars and stripes up a flagpole that towered higher than the stadium. A loud cheer followed the end of the anthem, but a deafening cheer greeted the Notre Dame players as they sprinted out of the tunnel under the north goal post, led by the thin and bespectacled coach, Lou Holtz. To Mary Alice, the coach looked something like Mr. Lackey.

The Stanford players ran out on the field under a chorus of boos. The whole scene was pretty exciting for

Mary Alice. She was feeling like she did at Christmas time, waiting in anticipation, wondering what wonderful event would happen next.

There was a buzz among the fans as both teams lined up for the opening kickoff. The buzz turned into cheers as the Notre Dame speedster Rocket Ismail gathered in the kickoff on the ten, swiftly running the ball out to the thirty-six yard line. Mary Alice's heart fluttered as her hero quarterback Tony Rice, rushed for twelve yards. Then she remembered what Mr. Lackey said about watching the game; she started to go up and down the aisles hawking the programs. But every now and then she would peek down to see what Tony was doing.

"Programs…get your programs!" Mary Alice shouted as she moved up and down the aisles. The fans were more intent on watching the game than in buying programs, so Mary Alice didn't sell very many.

She spotted a fan wearing a long black hooded sweatshirt, sitting on an end seat about ten rows in front of her, looking her way. The fan stretched out an arm and beckoned for her to come close. A chance to sell a program! Mary Alice quickly went down the steep steps, and as she got closer, she noticed the fan's face was completely concealed under the hood. That seemed odd! She slowed down, approaching this disturbing looking person feeling a little jumpy.

"Do… you… want a …program?" she stammered. That was when Mary Alice looked directly into the black hood, and what she saw gave her the shivers. All she could see were deep wells with empty sockets. The black hooded person reached toward her and touched her hand. Cold. So very cold. Mary Alice instinctively withdrew her hand,

and just then the roar of the crowd made her look down on the field. Tony Rice had just run thirty yards for a touchdown! Pandemonium erupted. Mary Alice joined in the cheering, and when she looked back, the black hooded person was gone.

The game ended with Notre Dame winning 42-14. Mary Alice turned in the last of her programs to Mr. Lackey, and he gave her twenty bucks as her pay. She joined the happy Notre Dame fans that were spilling out of the stadium; she was on her way to meet her dad at Washington Hall, a campus theater, where he had to set up some chairs or something before going home. As she walked along on the crowded campus sidewalks, she couldn't get her mind off that strange black hooded fan, and then she thought of all the abnormal occurrences in her life right then.

"What is happening to me?" she said out loud to no one.

▼

## CHAPTER SIX

"What are you so mad about?" Mary Alice angrily asked her dad. "Notre Dame won."

She was standing with her hands on her hips in the lobby of Washington Hall. Chuck Gallegan was furious as he carried chairs into a storage room. Every now and then he would fling one against a wall.

Mary Alice glared at him. "Notre Dame didn't beat the spread, am I right?"

Chuck didn't answer. He flung another chair.

"How much did you lose? One hundred? Two Hundred? Am I getting close?" Mary Alice stared at the floor, the anger blazing in her eyes.

Chuck Gallegan said nothing. He didn't have to. Mary Alice knew the answer. He lost big time again.

A tear splashed on the parquet floor, then another. Mary Alice couldn't stop crying. Trying to hide the tears from her dad, she knuckled her eyes with her fists, but it didn't help much.

"I'm just going to walk home," she mumbled. Turning around, she was out the front door in a hurry. Her dad did nothing to stop her.

The day had grown to dark. The outside air was fresh and clean. Wispy clouds were passing over a half moon. Bright stars were shining brightly, even in the glow of the campus lights. Still, Mary Alice continued to feel let down.

Why was she so disappointed? Her dad was a chronic gambler; she would just have to accept it. That was all there was to it. Why fight it?

Sobbing again, she started to walk to the back of Washington Hall. She did not want anyone to see a blubbering idiot.

Washington Hall is a very old theater, built in the last century after a devastating campus fire. The numbers 1881 are neatly engraved high on the outside wall of the traditional brick building. There are gothic spires and eye catching gargoyles, giving the theater a rather spooky looking appearance.

Mary Alice paused in front of a high set of metal steps leading up to the building's back door. A few yards away from the steps was an outdoor hand-pump, and next to the pump was a statue of a crown-bedecked king holding a scepter and a model of Sacred Heart, the campus church. Wanting to wash her face, Mary Alice wandered over to the pump, and as she pressed down on the handle, eerie fog rose out from a cluster of bushes. Strangely, the fog began to take a ghostly human shape. Mary Alice stepped back. The misty phantom floated right by her head before she could see it was the splitting image of a young man riding large white horse. The man gave Mary Alice a lopsided grin, and then he steered the horse straight up the steps, rearing high at the summit before passing through the solid doublewide door.

What was that? Mary Alice closed her eyes and opened them again. No sign of the white horse and rider. Her blood froze. Was that a ghost? Again, there are no such things as ghosts. But yet…

She just wanted to go home and climb under the covers of her nice warm bed. Perhaps the image had been a hallucination, she was way past exhausted. Ricardo had claimed he had once seen a leprechaun after staying up all night—yeah, that was it—the whole thing had been her weary brain dreaming while she was awake.

Mary Alice turned away from Washington Hall and started to jog. She decided take a shortcut home, even though it meant going through Cedar Grove, the age-old cemetery located on the southern edge of the campus. Her jog turned quickly into a run until she stopped in front of the fence that surrounded the Warren Golf Course. She would have to get across the golf course to reach the burial ground. Always feeling daring, Mary Alice gripped a fence post with both hands, carefully lifting herself up. She then swung her left tennis shoe over the top only to catch it on the wire. She hung there awkwardly before getting her other shoe over, but it too stuck in the fence. Upside down, she took a quick look around. Nobody seemed to be watching her. Good thing, she was embarrassed getting stuck like that. It took a lot of tugging to free her shoes, but after getting them loose, she fell to the other side with a thud. Fortunately for her, she broke no bones, so she slowly got to her feet and set off into the darkness.

The golf course was hilly and uneven. In the dark, it was hard to tell where she was going. She tripped a few times which made her slow to a shuffle. At the far side of the course, she saw it, the fence that separated the fairway from the cemetery. There was a man-sized rift in the fence, plenty big enough for her to slip through; she had gone through this opening many times before. Mary Alice hurried through and found herself a little downhill from the monuments of the dead.

Mary Alice paused to catch her breath. She looked around. There were tombstones and mausoleums spread throughout the well cared for cemetery. Most were tall in statue and very old, going back more than a hundred years. Names of many of the early settlers of South Bend were etched on the stones, a proud tribute to those who had come before.

This was the first time Mary Alice was in the cemetery after dark. It was so different, with misty shadows all around her. She was use to passing this way in the daylight when these grounds were clear and peaceful, but now the hard to see tombstones gave her a jittery feeling that she could not shake.

It would have been better for her not to come though Cedar Grove, she knew that, but if she didn't, she would have to go all the way around the campus to reach Notre Dame Avenue. And Notre Dame Avenue was the only way for her to leave the campus. This way was so much shorter. Then all she would have to do was cross Angela Boulevard and she would be home in a matter of minutes.

Where was the paved driveway that led out of the cemetery? There, in front of her, about thirty yards away. Mary Alice twisted her head violently back and forth, looking for any sign of trouble. Seeing nothing out of the ordinary, she started to carefully make her way toward the driveway. Not far to go.

Suddenly, she heard a piercing shriek directly over her head. She dove behind a tombstone, trying to hide behind it, but the stone wasn't all that large. A big black bird landed on the grass at her side, a crow or maybe a raven. The bird pecked at the ground a bit before it took flight, cawing as it flew away.

Mary Alice stood in the mist and smiled, a little self-conscious. So that was it, just a night bird. It seemed so funny. She was afraid of a bird? But then she remembered the poem she had to read in American Lit class last year written by that crazy Edger Allen Poe guy. "Quote the raven, nevermore." She remembered that line. Wait a minute! Wasn't the raven in the poem an omen of bad things to come? How about the big black bird she just saw? She didn't think it was so funny anymore.

Shivering just a little, she began to walk again. The night air was cooling rapidly, and the nylon jacket she was wearing wasn't enough to keep her warm. Then again, maybe she was shivering because she was a little bit nervous—and scared.

The open cemetery gates were just ahead. A little further.

Instantly the gate clanged shut. Mary Alice ran to the gate and furiously shook the metal bars. The gate wouldn't budge. In a panic, she started to climb the slippery horizontal bars and that was when something grabbed her from behind.

# CHAPTER SEVEN

▼

The hand, or claw that grabbed her was slimy feeling, and scaly, like a reptile. Mary Alice slipped away by going down on all fours. She knew she should be up and running, there was no time to waste, but her legs wouldn't obey her own command. It was better to just stay there in a crouch, spreading what little body heat she had left into the ground, wishing to make her shivering body invisible.

There was a banshee cry above her head, and that got her going. She was off and running. Something was right behind her, flying quicker than she could run. Staggering to a stop, and then ducking, she avoided being hit by the thing. As it zoomed past, she saw it, a black creature that looked like a serpent. A sulfurous stench took the place of the air. She had to find a place to hide.

A mausoleum was to her right. There was a ledge halfway up, and with the nearby street glow Mary Alice had just enough light to see there might be enough room to crawl in. She lunged forward and threw herself into the ledge, shoulders first, sliding, her tennis shoes finally making it safely inside.

The serpent reached in after her. It ripped at her shoes, almost tearing one off; somehow she managed to keep it on. She kicked, and kicked again, feeling a little numbness in her foot. Struggling for breath, she pushed and wriggled, forcing herself deeper into the ledge. She noticed the hideous creature had no arms or hands; it had been getting after her with wide-fanged jaws. It jabbed at her again and again before finally emitting a high warbling scream and flying away. Not very far though. Mary Alice could see it hovering outside the ledge, waiting for her to come out. Fat chance of that happening.

The flying serpent would not leave. It swooped around the mausoleum like a restless bird of prey seeking its next meal. Mary Alice wasn't worried about the serpent flying near her head. She was more concerned about her legs, which were beginning to feel like bricks since she couldn't move them much inside the cramped quarters of the ledge.

Then, just when she didn't think she could hold out much longer, she noticed the serpent wasn't in view. It had flown away. Mary Alice didn't hesitate. She crawled out of the ledge, placing her feet gingerly on the ground. Pins and needles shot up and down her legs. A few minutes of vigorous rubbing would get her legs ready to run again.

The feeling in her legs was coming back. She looked up. There, standing between two tombstones, was a shadowy hooded figure. So familiar. Wait a minute! It was the mysterious fan, the hooded person she saw in the stadium!

There was the serpent wrapped around his shoulders; Mary Alice could just make it out in the darkness. The serpent let out an ear-shattering shriek, but the hooded person comforted it, caressing its putrid back. The shrieking stopped.

Slowly, the hooded person turned his head toward Mary Alice. Raising his right arm, the person extended a finger in her direction, seeming to point at something on her body, her heart maybe.

Mary Alice felt a profound urge to run away. But she could not move. It was like she was under the spell of the hooded person, like she was one of those zombies on the late night scary movies. Her heart froze as she became more immobile.

The person was trying to communicate with her; he was trying to get in her mind. She could hear his voice as one does in a dream, he was saying, "go now, but we will meet again, and when we do, you will be mine."

It was a full minute before Mary Alice was freed from the spell of the hooded person. There was no time to be scared. She took off running, past the hooded person, past the flying serpent, back the way she had come, back to the golf course. She never looked to see if she was being chased.

This time Mary Alice scaled the golf course fence without any trouble. Washington Hall was where she wanted to be, behind the building's secure walls, to find her dad; she didn't know where else to go.

The heavy Washington Hall front door slammed shut with a bang as Mary Alice stepped inside.

"Dad…Dad…where are you?"

Mary Alice was frantic. No one was around. No sign of her dad anywhere.

"Dad… can you hear me?"

No answer.

"Does he even know I'm here?" she wondered out loud.

Mary Alice felt a twinge of loneliness. He was never there when she really needed him. If she were burning in a house fire, would he go in and try to pull her out of the flames? How about if she was drowning? Would he, or anyone else for that matter, jump in the water to try to save her? Not likely! Nobody cared that much about her.

Sniveling, she backed up against a wall and slid down to a sitting position. One solitary tear fell down a cheek, getting into her mouth, tasting bitter. Just like the way she felt.

She held her head with both hands, hardly breathing. Everything she could see began to spin around and around, the walls, chairs, windows, faster, faster; the whole world was tumbling out of control. Mary Alice closed her eyes. She never intended to open them again.

"Hey kiddo!"

Dumb with fear, Mary Alice looked up. Did someone say something to her? Was she hearing voices?

"Over here!"

Mary Alice glanced to her right. There, hovering in midair was the head of a young man with dark hair, fair brown eyes, and a lopsided grin. No body, just a head.

"Well, that's it, I've finally gone crazy," she said to herself. Then she did something very peculiar. She started to laugh.

"What's so funny, kiddo?" the head asked, his face glowing. "Haven't you ever seen a talking head before?"

Mary Alice didn't say anything. What could she say? First there was the flying serpent, then the threatening hooded person, and now a talking head. She would just keep her mouth shut.

The head smiled. "I'll tell you what," he said, "I think you would feel better if I had a full body."

Broad shoulders, a narrow waist, and long legs materialized from out of his head. A lean muscled six feet tall man stood in front of Mary Alice. She slowly inched her way up but still kept her back to the wall. Her eyes widened. "Who…who are you?"

The young man bowed at the waist. "George is the name and haunting is my game."

"Haunting…"

"Yes, that's right, what you see before you is a first class one hundred percent grade A ghost."

"Wait a minute," Mary Alice said, her heart pounding in her chest. "You're the man I saw on the white horse riding up the steps!"

"Yeah, that was me. I love to make a glorious first impression. I get a lot of mileage out of that horse. We have been making appearances around here for several years now."

Oh great, she was seeing ghosts! But she couldn't help it; ghost or not, she found herself really taking a liking to this young man with the lopsided grin. She even felt a little playful. "Don't ghosts rattle chains and moan and carry on something awful?" she asked with a smile of her own.

"Just in "The Christmas Carol" and bad horror stories," the young man replied. "But I can screech bloody murder if you like."

"No, that's quite all right," Mary Alice said, shivering. "I'll take your word for it."

"Now, there is a reason I am appearing in front of you," he said.

"What? Why…"

"I have come from the Ghost World to give you a warning, and help you if I can."

"The Ghost World? What is that?"

"The Ghost World…" George began to explain, but then his legs disappeared. He blinked twice and his legs were back in place. He cleared his throat and began to talk again. "The Ghost World is a place where people go after they die who feel they are not yet ready for Heaven."

Okay, this was getting to be a little too much. But even if all this was a bad dream, or a weird hallucination, Mary Alice decided to go along with it. "How could anyone not be ready for Heaven?" she asked.

George's head began to lift off his shoulders, but he quickly placed both hands on top and pushed his head back in place. He didn't miss a beat. "Some people feel their lives were incomplete, or they feel a living loved one still needs them; oh, there are a lot of reasons."

"Oh." Mary Alice was impressed. Then she was confused. "How about you? Why aren't you in Heaven?

"I'm not sure," George said, his lopsided grin pinching a little. "I'm supposed to help you, I guess."

"I think I better sit down," Mary Alice said, letting out a big sigh. She sat cross-legged in the middle of the lobby, smacked dab on the clean parquet floor.

"Anyway," George continued, "I do know this. The hooded person you saw twice today is shadowing you; he wants you for something evil."

"How do you know this?"

"Not sure. It has something to do with your father's gambling. Don't look so surprised, I know all about his gambling sickness. What I can tell you is that the hooded person may be trying to get to him through you."

What would he want with my dad?

"I couldn't say," George said, for the first time talking in a serious tone. "He might want to take him to the underworld, the place of lost souls."

Mary Alice's face turned a beat red. "What…what can we do?"

"Well," George laughed, "there is going to be a new kid in your class on Monday, and that new kid will be me."

There was the sound of two men talking to each other coming from the top of the balcony. Mary Alice recognized the voices of her dad and Rick, another campus worker. The two men were coming down the stairs. She got to her feet to greet them.

"Here's my dad now," Mary Alice said, spinning around to face George, but he had disappeared.

"I see you've come back, Kitten," Chuck Gallegan said. "Ready to go home?"

"Yea, I'm ready dad." She decided not to say anything about George or about what happened in the graveyard. Maybe she would find out more about these curious happenings on Monday, from the new kid in class.

## CHAPTER EIGHT

▼

"Good morning boys and girls," Sister Barbara Ann cheerfully said to the class. "We have a new student with us today. Say hello to George."

"Hello George," the class repeated in a silly singsong voice.

There was no mistaking it, Mary Alice realized. The boy in front of the class was the ghost she had seen and talked to on Saturday night. He was a younger boy, and shorter, the size of a normal thirteen year old, but he had the same curly hair and most importantly the same lopsided grin.

George waved to the class and headed for the empty desk directly behind Mary Alice, and as he walked past her, he gave her a sly wink.

It was recess before she had a chance to talk to George. They were tossing a football to each other, trying to move away from the other kids. Mary Alice had a scowl on her face. George seemed real all right, and that was why it was so difficult for Mary Alice to keep in mind she was talking to a ghost.

George leaned toward her and threw the football a little harder. "What's the matter? I've never seen such a long face on a young girl."

To avoid meeting his eyes, Mary Alice cradled the ball after catching it. For a moment she just stood there, feeling prickles tickling the back of her neck. Then she casually tossed the ball back to George before speaking. "Tell me everything you know about the connection between the hooded person and my dad."

George shrugged. "I really don't know much more than you do. We have to find a Mr. Bumblebee; he will tell us more. Do you know such a man?"

"Mr. Bumblebee? Mr. Jack Bumblebee? Why, he's the janitor at our school."

"Well, we have to talk to him, the sooner the better."

"But he's really strange. Never talks to the kids, or the teachers. It's like he lives in another world."

"I think," said George, "that is why we need to talk to him."

"I have a game tomorrow after school, maybe after that we can go to his house or something."

"Oh, that's right, you're a girl quarterback," George said with a chuckle. His eyes began to sparkle.

"And what's the matter with that!" Mary Alice said hotly.

"Well, in my day, girls wore calico dresses and spent their time making cookies or Yankee pot roast."

"Well, this is the 1980's buster; girls can do anything boys can do."

Mary Alice noticed her right hand was balled into a fist. Was she going to have to sock a Ghost?

"Hooray for you," George shouted. "I like a girl who sticks up for herself."

Just then the afternoon bell rang, summoning the children back to class. George took the football, stepped back two feet, and punted the ball high and far.

Mary Alice watched the ball in flight and whistled. "George, that ball went about sixty yards. Did you ever play football?

"A little bit," George said between clenched teeth. "But that was a long time ago."

They were both quiet as they walked into the school. Mary Alice, lost in her thoughts, wanted nothing to do with Jack Bumblebee. Sadly for her, saving her dad from the clutches of the evil hooded person would involve dealing with some really strange characters. Thank goodness that George, a friendly ghost, was by her side to help shoulder the load.

The Tuesday afternoon game against the Saint John Bosco Titans came so fast Mary Alice had scant time to worry about how she could help her dad. It didn't affect her play even a little. She threw three touchdown passes, and ran for another one, leading her team to a twenty eight point half time lead.

Speedy Billy Barton for Our Lady gathered in the second half kickoff and brought the ball back to the thirty-five. After two running plays that only gained four yards, Coach Mike sent Todd Hertel in as a flanker with the next play.

"Coach wants thirty-four wide," Todd told Mary Alice. This would be a screen pass to the fullback. Mary Alice called the play—the ball was snapped—Tommy Jones snagged the short pass—and was tackled for a five-yard loss. Coach Mike was livid as Mary Alice ran off the field; Todd Hertel stayed in to do the punting.

"What you doing," he screamed into Mary Alice's face. "That's not the play I called!"

"But coach…"

"I don't want to hear any excuses, Mary Alice. I'm the coach of this team and I call the plays. Now go sit down on the bench and think about it. Todd's going in as quarterback next series."

Her head down, Mary Alice slowly walked over to the side of the bench. George was standing there, watching the game.

"What happened?" George asked.

"I'm…I'm not sure. Coach said I ran the wrong play."

Then it dawned on her. Todd gave her the wrong signals on purpose, knowing that an angry Coach Mike would yank her out of the game. This way, Todd would get to play quarterback. When she explained all this to George, his face lit up like a Christmas tree. "Well, we'll just have to see how this Mr. Hertel does when he is in the game," he said gleefully.

Sure enough, an Our Lady safety intercepted a pass and Todd came in as quarterback. The first play was a straight handoff to the fullback that gained five yards. Next, an incomplete pass. Third down. Todd Hertel went back to pass, pump faked, eluded a tackler and headed down the far sidelines. He was in the clear.

Mary Alice looked over at George—who waved his right arm in Todd's direction. Running as fast as he could, Todd was certain to score. But then the unbelievable happened. Thirty yards from the goal line, Todd's gold football pants began to fall down, first to his knees, then to his ankles. He still tried to run, but he was reduced to a pathetic shuffle. The spectators roared with laughter. Even Sister Barbara Ann was laughing, but blushing too before averting her eyes. The funniest part was the sight of Todd's underwear—red hearts on white boxer shorts.

Two John Bosco defenders quickly caught up with Todd and tackled him before he could go five more yards. Todd's dad ran out into the field, hoping to help his son pull his pants back up, and as they tugged and jerked together, George's arm went up again. This time, to the crowd's amusement, Mr. Hertel's tan corduroy pants also fell down—and he had on matching red hearts on white boxer shorts. Father and son pulled mightily on their pants, but nothing doing.

Hopping off the field, the two thoroughly embarrassed Hertels gradually made their way to the far end of the small grandstand, stumbling every few feet, still trying everything they could to get their pants back up. Mary Alice glared at George. She knew he had something to do with this hilarity because Todd's lopsided grin was in full fashion.

The only one not amused by the Hertel's predicament was Coach Mike. The rough-hewed coach was all about football, didn't tolerate anything else. "Gallegan, take over for Hertel," he hollered and just like that Mary Alice was the quarterback again. After the game ended, an easy Our Lady triumph, she searched for George, but he had vanished. She wasn't worried; she knew in her heart of hearts she would see him in school the next day. But what happened to the Hertels? An hour after the game, they were still struggling with their pants.

# CHAPTER NINE

▼

Todd Hertel pedaled his red Schwinn bicycle exactly in the middle of curvy Riverside Drive. A car spun around him, honking with a lot of anger. The blonde longhaired boy paid little attention to the driver; he had other things on his mind. He had not forgotten the previous day's shame. All those people laughing as he and his dad yanked on their pants like a couple of two year olds. Laughing at them. Nobody laughs at the Hertels.

Mary Alice had to be behind all this humiliation. Sure he had given her the wrong play. How else would he get to play quarterback? His dad was always whining: how come you're not the quarterback Todd, how can you let a girl beat you out Todd, what's next Todd, are you going to sing in the choir? Too much pressure. He must take his revenge.

That new kid in class, what's his name, George something or other, he seemed to be friendly with Mary Alice all fully quick. What's the connection? Todd was determined to find out.

A brown UPS truck came around the next corner. The truck slowed down to keep from hitting Todd head-on. The driver, a balding middle-aged man with a dirty mustache, was boiling over mad. He shook his fist at Todd, but it did no good, Todd just kept on going, oblivious to all around him.

The Saint Joseph River, on Todd's right, determined the shape of the road. That explained the many curves, some at almost a ninety-degree angle. With the splendid view of the colorful fall foliage, Riverside Avenue was a scenic way to travel to the north side of town. But none of this concerned Todd; Pinhook Park was his destination.

Pinhook Park once featured a sandy beach on a tributary of the river, but the sand was now overgrown with wild grass and weeds. The muddy water used to be clear, and was a great place for a swim. Not anymore. Too dangerous. Only fisherman could be found here, trolling for carp. Todd wasn't interested in casting a hook; he came here for one reason, to get away from home.

Todd was getting madder and madder as he pedaled. It was always his dad. He expected his son to be totally excellent. Constantly interfering with his life. Todd could not do anything without his dad putting in his two cents worth. Do as I say. And if Todd doesn't? Sent to bed with no supper. Or grounded. No TV for a week. So many ways to punish. Todd had no choice. Play baseball, basketball, football—and you better be the best. It was like his dad was trying to live his live over again through his son.

Mom was no help. Mrs. Hertel went along with everything the Mr. commanded, as if she was frightened of him. The anger that filled Todd's heart spilled over on those soft and helpless enough to come across his path. Was he a bully? Yeah. In spite of everything, he loved his dad. He didn't want to hurt or disappoint him, he would never confront him, so he vented his anger on those he perceived weaker than himself. Or on those who got in the way of the goals his dad had set for him. And presently, the person most in his way was Mary Alice.

He first ran into her athletic abilities at a Punt, Pass, and Kick competition the previous year. This event, held every spring at Boland Park, tested the abilities of the kid contestants on their punting, passing and kicking abilities. Distance and accuracy were judged most important. Todd had won his age division the last two years, easily. But in the state finals, he had lost, much to his and especially his dad's chagrin. And the most disappointing part was the state winners get to go on the field at the halftime of a Colt's game in Indianapolis. A trophy presentation on live TV! Todd wanted this recognition in the worst way. That would surely make his dad proud!

And along came Mary Alice to ruin his singular ambition. In his last year of eligibly, Todd was out-punted, out-passed, and out-kicked by that girl every way imaginable. Todd's dad never got over this slight, never got over his son losing to a girl. More nagging. More finger pointing. More strain on their relationship. Mary Alice won the state championship and was on TV. He never would be. That was the trigger, the start of Todd's hatred for Mary Alice. Maybe this was also the beginning of his sorry self-hatred.

Arriving at the park a little before dusk, Todd parked his Schwinn at a bike stand and eased on down to the water's edge. Shivery goose bumps ran up and down his arms. He had on a lightweight tee shirt, wished he had brought along a windbreaker. Well, he would rather freeze than be at home with his messed up parents.

Something flew over Todd's head as he skipped rocks on the stilled water. Something long and black. That got his attention. He peered up into the semi-darkness. Nothing.

"Do you want to get even?"

Todd turned around to see a man standing next to a boat launch. The man had on a long black hooded sweatshirt.

"Do you want to get even?"

The hooded man was speaking to him, yet Todd couldn't hear any spoken words, the man seemed to be putting the words in the center of his mind.

"Who are you?" Todd asked, wondering if he even needed to talk out loud in order for the man to understand.

"Your friend," the man said thru thought.

"My friend? I don't know you."

"I can help you get even with Mary Alice," the man spoke-thought. "She has made your life miserable. I can help you fix that."

Todd wished he could make out the man's face, but the hood and the descending darkness made it impossible to see eyes, nose, or a mouth.

"I can help you," the hooded man repeated in a thought tone like a harsh cold wind over an open grave.

"You can't help me," Todd said, starting to get a little scared.

"Give me your anger, and your fear, and I will do the rest."

"How can I do that?"

"Come closer."

Todd didn't want to move, yet, there he was, standing directly in front of the hooded man. There was a sucking sound, and the air came out of Todd's open mouth, knocked out of him. The air broke into milky ropes, drifting into the hooded man's face, or where his face ought to be. Then, the man dissolved, becoming a heavy mist hanging in the cool air. The mist moved over the water until it was lost from view. Todd was left standing alone, by the water's edge, looking at nothing.

He couldn't gather a breath until his breath came back in a loud gasp. His heart was pounding so hard his temples were vibrating. An owl hooted. A church bell rang.

"Who was that?" Todd thought. His head hurt and he wanted to go home. Glancing at the night sky, he couldn't see any stars. It was like he was stranded in a black vacuum. He immediately jumped on his bike.

This time he kept off the middle of Riverside Drive. Heat rushed through him and he felt the urge to cry. He never did that and he would not do it now. Crying was for sissies. He began to pedal faster, noticing for the first time the odor of rotting leaves intermingling with the fishy smell of the river. He had never felt so afraid.

▼

## CHAPTER TEN

"People say he shoots unwanted visitors."

Mary Alice and George were walking up the crumbling concrete steps that fronted Mr. Jack Bumblebee's beige bungalow house. She was telling George barely above a whisper all she knew about the school's janitor. "I think the nuns feel sorry for him, that's why he's got the janitor's job. Some say he's an escape convict. I've heard even worse. I've heard he's a vampire. I don't believe that. There is no such thing as vampires or…"

"Or ghosts," George said quickly.

"Yea, well I never used to believe in ghosts."

Within a few feet of the front door, Mary Alice stood still for a moment, took a deep breath and slowly moved forward. She seized the door knocker and rapped it three times. The door knocker was shaped like a skull.

Nobody answered the door. "Looks like he's not home, let's go," Mary Alice said, stepping back.

George looked around suspiciously. "No, he's in there. I can feel it. Just wait, he's coming."

At last there was a squealing noise and the door opened. Mr. Bumblebee was not there.

Mary Alice bent over and peeked around the corner, George holding on to her shoulder in case there was a need to pull her back out of the way of a monster or something. She turned and whispered, "I don't see anybody."

George took a look for himself. It was gloomy inside, empty and quiet. There was a bare light bulb in the vestibule, just bright enough to show a hallway. Moving rapidly, George glided by Mary Alice, his feet not touching the floor. "Come on in," he told her. "It seems safe enough."

Mary Alice followed him in. "Well, what should we do now?" she asked.

Before he could respond, George soared straight up, his head almost touching the ten foot high ceiling, hanging in the air as if he was a balloon. "Grab my legs and pull me down," he hollered.

"What are you doing up there," Mary Alice asked, giving him a cold-eyed stare. She reached for a foot and brought him back to the grimy wood finished floor. George was as light as a feather.

"Wasn't my idea," George said, surprised. "Something about this house is making me lose my ability to remain solid. You're going to have to help me keep grounded."

Mr. Jack Bumblebee still had not made an appearance. In a way this pleased Mary Alice, for Jack Bumblebee was a bent figure, face thin and drawn, bony arms and legs—a very scary looking person. She really did not want to meet him.

"Let's go down the hall," George said. Mary Alice nodded, and took out of her jean's pocket a tiny pen size flashlight she always carried with her. She flicked the flashlight on, and held it out at arm length, illuminating ever so slightly the hall's narrow tattered walls.

"You know," George muttered, "this place is scaring me, and that's hard to say for a ghost."

Mary Alice at first didn't know what George was talking about, but then she began to nervously chuckle, picturing a ghost afraid of his own shadow.

They proceeded down the drafty hall, Mary Alice walking but George still gliding. She had to hold tightly onto his hand to keep him from rising to the ceiling. The hall didn't figure to be very far, after all, the house was a bungalow, a cozy cottage at best. But several minutes went by and there still was no end in sight.

Mary Alice took a long look at George. "Should we keep on going?"

"I...I guess so," the ghost said uncertainly, but as he spoke, a fiery red glow cast light upon them. The light showed they were in a large, palace size room. They stood fast, not sure what to do next, and as they thought it over, a deep voice came straight out of the glow shouting "you're getting warmer!"

"What did he say?" Mary Alice asked George under her breath. He turned to her and shrugged.

"I said you're getting warmer!" the voice shouted again.

Instantly a heavy set man moved in from the red glow, riding a long broom as if he was a witch. A flowing gown of many sparkling colors fell over his shoulders. His round hairless cheeks were ruddy and his eyes flashed—all this made a lantern of his face. A cone shaped wizard hat covered with several half-moons and stars fit snuggly atop his head.

"Welcome to my home," he said pleasantly, coming to a stop at Mary Alice's and George's feet. "Jack Bumblebee here, hoping for your approval."

The ghost and the girl stared at each other, their mouths wide open.

Jack Bumblebee stepped away from the broom, clapping his hands, making the broom disappear. "I've been waiting for you to come see me; I have much to tell you two."

"But...but you're an old..." Mary Alice was trying to talk but the words were not coming out properly.

Raising his eyebrows, Jack Bumblebee said, "That's all right, young lady. You've seen me at school as a decrepit old man that has trouble standing upright. This, my dear, is the real me."

Mary Alice gave him a scornful look.

"Let me explain further, my dear," Jack bellowed. "The old man you see at school is how I look outside this house. But the way I look now, full bodied, is how I really am. Now does this make sense to you two?"

George and Mary Alice shook their heads no.

Jack Bumblebee snapped his fingers and three wingback chairs appeared. "Sit down, my dears, and let me explain. I would wager you two would like some hot tea."

He snapped his fingers again, and three piping hot cups of tea materialized on top of a small dinette table. Jack reached for a cup and raised it to his lips.

"Ah, there is nothing like a hot cup of tea," he said, wiping his mouth with a sleeve. "Now, as you two probably have surmised, I am not a mortal. Some would call me a wizard, but I prefer to call myself an intermediary—an envoy between this world and the next."

"But at school you are a janitor," Mary Alice said, passing a cup of tea to George. She was glad to have something liquid, her mouth was so dry she could hardly speak.

"Yes," Jack said, "the nuns have been very kind to me. You see, I need this house for my calling, and I need a job to pay the mortgage. When one resides in the mortal world, one has to live by their rules."

"What is the purpose of this house?" George asked, keeping a foot under the chair rung to keep from drifting.

"Well, I guess you would say this house is haunted, but it's haunted for a reason." Jack said. He took another sip of tea. "Now, now my precious dears—don't look so bewildered. Every now and then an evil spirit escapes from underneath the Ghost World and it's my job to get them back."

Mary Alice let out her breath. "The hooded person…"

"Yes, that's right," Jack told her, "the hooded person you encountered in the cemetery is the criminal Sam Ridge. And the flying serpents you have seen are his soul catchers, the extension of his evil soul."

How do we fit in?" asked Mary Alice.

"Yeah," said George. "I'm a ghost and I can't figure this one out."

"I need your help, the both of you," Jack said, leaning back against the chair. "Sam Ridge, a murderer in life, has come back to the mortal world to seek revenge for his execution. I know he is in this town, and Mary Alice, I believe he is after your father."

"But…but why?" Mary Alice stammered.

"He feeds on fear and hate, takes it out of the souls that allow their bad feelings to take over their lives, and your dad, with his gambling, is a prime candidate to be his next victim."

"My dad says gambling is fun, says it is not a problem—"

"My dear, when gambling is obsessive, as it is for your father, well, he doesn't know how to stop making bets, even when he keeps losing. Now this scares him, and makes him hate himself and everyone around him, even you."

George's foot slipped off the chair rung and once again he began to float. Mary Alice pulled him back down.

"In this house, George, you are under ghost rules," Jack said with a wheezy laugh. He sat upright, yawned, and stretched his arms. "Now here is the problem, my young dears. Every bit of a miserable soul that Sam Ridge breathes in makes him stronger, and if he gets strong enough, he can't be returned to the Ghost World. He would become immortal, his evil never to end."

"How can we stop him?" George asked before Mary Alice could.

"Sam Ridge thinks he can get to your dad through you, Mary Alice. So, you are the key to finishing him off. And George, this is where you come in. You must take Mary Alice into the Ghost World to find Sam Ridge's living crystal quartzite."

Looking thoughtful, Mary Alice asked, "What is the living crystal quartzite?"

"Ah, the living crystal," Jack said with a sigh. "Each living person is assigned the brilliant crystal when they are born, as clear as the cleanest glass. If a person does good deeds in their life, the crystal remains clean and clear, but if they do evil things, the crystal darkness."

The blood drained from Mary Alice's face.

"Wow, you're as pale as one of us ghosts," George told her, and then he asked Jack, "How can a mortal go into the Ghost World."

"There is only one time of the year that a mortal can enter—and that is All Hallows Eve—a week from today. You must take her, George; the portal to the Ghost World is in the basement of Washington Hall, and for better or worse that is your haunting grounds."

"But why do I have to go!" cried Mary Alice. "Why can't you capture Sam Ridge and return him to your Ghost World?"

"You see how I look outside this house—a walking skeleton. I have no power or strength as a mortal. You must bring him to this house, and then I can see that he is returned to where he belongs."

Jack Bumblebee got to his feet and snapped his fingers. The broomstick reappeared. "It's up to you, Mary Alice. Only you can save your dad."

Bowing her head, Mary Alice made every effort not to cry. It all sounded so horrible.

"Oh, one more thing," Jack said. "When you take possession of Sam Ridge's crystal, you must show it to him so he can see his own reflection. An evil doer cannot face his own cowardly wretched face—only then can he be lured inside the crystal and then you can bring him to me."

"Do you mean he would physically be inside…" Mary Alice started to ask.

"Yes," Jack interrupted, "if you are successful, Sam Ridge will be your prisoner, shrunken and completely powerless."

The broomstick, with Jack Bumblebee astride it, lifted off the floor. "Good luck, my dears," Jack shouted, and he soared back into the red glow.

Alone again, Mary Alice and George were speechless. Mary Alice's palms were sweaty, so she wiped them on her jeans. Her legs felt limp, and her pulse pounded against her skull. Then, to her amazement, a door suddenly opened in the hallway wall where there was no door before. The ghost and the girl didn't hesitate; they quickly dashed through it—coming outside to the smoky scent of leaves burning in a pile.

"Did I just dream all that?" Mary Alice asked.

"I don't think so," George replied. "I saw it all too, and we ghosts don't ever dream."

"Whoa." Mary Alice trembled. "Well, we better get going. Looks like we gotta save my dad."

## CHAPTER ELEVEN

▼

Lately, she just was so very tired. Becky Gallegan was on her knees, scrubbing the linoleum floor with big sweeping motions, swishing the wet rag like a crazed painter on a massive canvas. Ever since she had left home and moved into the Green Bay YWCA, she was tired in general. Tired of the people around her. Tired of the banality of TV and the happy dance songs on the radio that reminded her of how life should be lived. She was tired of wishing everything was right, that it would all make sense. Maybe that was why she volunteered to scrub the floor, the physical action would ease the numbness she felt, the spent lack of hope.

She was a runaway, like the girl on that song she liked so much when she as a kid, the one by Del Shannon. The worst part was leaving her daughter, leaving Mary Alice at an age when she needed her most. Becky no longer could be around to watch her home be shattered by the gambling of her husband. That is why she left. She hoped it wouldn't be forever. But it might be.

She had first seen Chuck on the football field in high school, running for a touchdown, the fans on her side of the stands cheering him on, wanting to be him, even the girls, maybe because they were not allowed to play sports in that era of low expectations. They made an odd couple around school—Becky the serious student and Chuck who only lived for whatever sport were in season. There was something about Chuck that drew her close to him, and it took her awhile to figure out what it was. She was chatty while Chuck seemed to have problems putting a string of words together, losing his train of thought just when she thought he might be about to say something interesting. Falling asleep in movies. Always underneath his car, tinkering with something or other. Wouldn't read a book for a million dollars.

Yes, she finally knew why she wanted to be close to him. Through sports Chuck could attain immediate success, a touchdown run, a long basketball shot, a home run. Success came so easy to him, while Becky would have to study hard to do well on a test and who would care anyway. Hanging with Chuck, by being his girl, she could stand in the shadow of his success, the sport hero, and it gave her an identity she felt never would come to her any other way.

She had friends alright, but Chuck had no interest in them with their talk of boring movies and who was dancing with whom at the latest school dance. After her marriage to Chuck, her friends were left behind, a sacrifice for her love for Chuck, she thought, but maybe it was because she had become hard in her thinking, had lost her ability to see the best in people.

It was the gambling. Baseball and football games, cards, dice--you name it, Chuck would bet on it. Their marriage was fine their first few years, but she didn't know-- maybe he got bored, but the betting got more intensive every year, even after Mary Alice was born. Money troubles soon followed. Bills couldn't be paid. Creditors hounding at their door. She knew she still loved him, but she couldn't watch his self destruction anymore, so she left home.

Becky got up off her knees and went to a corner window and looked out to the street below. She watched as a woman of about her age walked slowly by, talking with a young woman, maybe her daughter, she thought. The young woman was a thin, and tall, like Mary Alice, maybe the girl played sports too. She wondered how the woman and the girl below her got along. Did they quarrel over stupid things, like clothes and make-up and what kind of boys the girl dates? Then Becky thought of Mary Alice, her daughter, how much she loves her, how much it hurts not to be with her, and she remembered the fights they used to have, the arguments over her playing sports with boys, especially football. Girls don't sweat and get dirty. What was she raising – a female Walter Payton? But she knew it was more than that. She was losing her daughter to Chuck, to the world of sports and gambling, and she was afraid she would never get her back.

There was phlegm in the back of her throat now, the tears coming down her face one at a time, splashing onto her blouse, leaving individual wet spots. A telephone! She must find a telephone!

She found one in an unlocked office on the second floor. But even when the phone rang on the other end of the line—even before the receiver was lifted to her daughter's ear—Becky knew that she would say nothing. That is the way it had been since the beginning of the year.

"Hello, this is the Gallegan residence."

Becky wanted to ask Mary Alice how she was doing, tell her how much she loves her, but the words wouldn't come, there was nothing between them but garbled talking coming from the family room television.

"Hello…hello…mom, is this you…"

Standing in the office, she waited a few precious seconds before putting the phone down, hearing the echo of her daughter's voice mixing with the thumping of her heart. Ringing silence then filled the office. It would torture her the rest of the day, the rest of the week, no doubt about that.

She had almost said before hanging up, "I'm coming home."

## Chapter Twelve

▼

The blackness of the heavy night sky pressed down, the nearby buildings closed in, everyone he passed were bad people that wanted to wring his neck.

Chuck Gallegan, walking slowly down Michigan Street with the whole world against him, leaped into the black hole of depression with all his might. Only minutes before, he'd been the big cheese, winning three straight games of pool at Mira's, the newest poolroom in town, five hundred on the plus side, but in one game he had lost it all, and after that, he didn't even have a dime to buy gas for his truck. So he walked.

The crumbling sidewalk seemed to turn into thick wet sand, and he was sinking fast. Leaving that poolroom with empty pockets made him realize he was a hopeless loser, stuck in the dungeon of his own making.

All he wanted was to be left alone, to figure things out, how did he get this way? His bleak life couldn't all be his fault. Passed over for promotions at work, which would have meant more money, yeah, that was part of his troubles. He just wanted for himself and his family the good things in life—which only money can provide. Gambling was just a means to an end; if he couldn't make money at work then placing bets would furnish him with his much desired wealth.

But there was more to it than that. The excitement of betting a lucky streak was a way out of his boring life. When he won, which wasn't often, he felt like his head was in the clouds. But then there was the other side. Losing made him feel lower than low. Then he would have to gamble as soon as he could to get that high in the sky feeling again.

And then there was the self-pity. His wife left him, she didn't make any attempt to understand him; didn't she know, he was just trying to give her a better life. Mary Alice? Chuck felt bad his little girl was in the middle of the family squabble. But she wasn't making much of an attempt to be in his corner either. She was always riding him about his gambling. Well, he didn't need either one of them.

He blinked out of his funk and found himself in O'Brien Park. What a dummy! He had walked in the wrong direction and was miles from his home. Well, he had better turn himself around, and soon too because it looked like one of those cold fall rains was not far away. Looking through a grove of trees, he saw a school building, dark and silent. He also saw somebody standing in front of the building, and then he didn't see him, must have gone inside. Maybe if he could find this person, he could ask for a ride home, if it wouldn't be too much of a bother.

The door of the school was not locked so Chuck went in. Kind of strange the front door of a school would be unlocked at night. Chuck figured the person he saw was the evening janitor. That would be okay, he could wait until the guy's work shift was over. Better than getting soaking wet.

"Hey, anybody here," Chuck shouted. No response.

"Can anybody hear me," he yelled again. His eyes had adjusted to the darkness. He could see a long corridor. But then he saw a shadow move quickly into what Chuck assumed was a classroom. He couldn't tell if it was a person, or if it was an animal, a large dog or perhaps a confused deer. Chuck had seen on the TV news about a deer that had crashed through a department store window. No broken glass here, though.

Mildly afraid, Chuck cursed his curiosity and crept down the corridor. On second thought, the shadow had to be the janitor, and he still needed a ride home.

"Hello!" Again, no one answered.

The school bell rang for no apparent reason. Actually, it was more of a buzz. The suddenness of this irritating noise made Chuck's heart leap to his throat, but at the same time he became aware of something long and black hurtling towards him. He followed his instincts and ducked, the thing just missing the top of his head.

Was that a bat? No, can't be, too long to be one of those flying rodents.

Crouching, Chuck peered through the darkness, expecting to be dive bombed again. But instead, he was lifted off the floor with a strong hand around his neck, slamming him against a wall.

Chuck's head rapped on concrete, momentarily bringing the darkness behind his eyes to the center of his skull. Blessedly, he gasped for breath and found it. The hand wasn't trying to choke him, just holding him in the air, two feet off the floor.

It was impossible to tell who was attacking him. All Chuck could see was a black hood covering a large head, the hood so deep that he could not make out a face. Staring into the emptiness of the hood, Chuck shrieked, "let me go!"

Kicking, and kicking again, Chuck's feet landed on a stout torso, but it was no good, he still could not free himself. But then the black hooded person flung Chuck to the floor.

Chuck didn't wait for a rematch; he was on his feet and out the door before his attacker could say boo. Hoping he wasn't being followed, Chuck raced down to Fellows Street and ran like he was being chased by the devil. It was raining in sheets, lightning flashing all around him, making it easy to pick him out in the dark night.

The black hooded person, Sam Ridge, stood outside the school door, caressing one of his soul catchers.

"See how he runs, scared out of his wits," he cackled as he flattened a hand on the slimy skin of the flying serpent. "He's not as afraid as I need him to be, but he is getting there. Soon he will lose all hope and faith. When he totally gives up on himself, he will be mine, and I will finally be too strong to ever be destroyed. I will have my vengeance."

He pulled down his hood, drinking in the rain. "Just a little more time," he snarled. "A little more time."

## Chapter Thirteen

▼

The championship game for the South Bend Intercity Catholic Football League was to be played on Sunday. The Our Lady Panthers were matched against the Saint Stephen Fire Cats.

With all that was going on with her dad, Mary Alice didn't feel much like playing football. George kept whispering in her ear to give the game her best shot. "There's nothing you can do for your dad until Halloween, so you need to keep yourself on a regular schedule," he finally said, dismissing her concerns with a wave of a hand. "Besides, your teammates need you to beat St. Vitus. You can't let them down."

Mary Alice thought about what she would do all week, and she finally decided George was giving sound advice. She would play the game to the best of her abilities. Beside, playing the game might get her mind off her troubles, at least for a while.

The funny thing was, at school the past few days, she would pass by the haggard Jack Bumblebee as he swept floors or cleaned windows, and she would say hi, but not once did he acknowledge her existence; it was as if they had never met. Maybe, she thought, they hadn't.

Game day turned out perfect, the kind of late October day that would make you think football is the sun's favorite sport. The Weather Channel said the afternoon temperature was 55 degrees, but in Northern Indiana that always meant it was warmer in the sun and cooler when the north wind whipped your way.

Mary Alice said good-bye to her dad and went outside. The wind hit her face with a mild slap. That was good. The breeze was strong enough to keep her from getting overheated but not so that her forward passes would sail. For her, it was a pinpoint passing day.

Chuck Gallegan told his daughter he would come to the game later. Claimed he had some errands to run. Of course, Mary Alice was not fooled. No doubt he put money down on pro football cards, and he would be stopping by his gambling bookie to see how his bets were doing. He probably had a wager on her game to boot.

Sighing, Mary Alice decided to take the long way. The game was to be played at the Marian High School field, with well cut grass and metal bleachers and a brightly lighted scoreboard, although the numbers would be hard to make out in the brilliant sun. No matter, the game would feel just like the big time.

Riding her mother's old rusty girl style bike, the kind with no bar in the middle, Mary Alice was in no hurry; she had left home two hours early. It felt kind of good to push the pedals of the old bike. The hard effort it took to keep the bike from toppling was a good way to get her legs ready for the game, to get the morning stiffness out of her joints.

It was nice to be alone, at least for a while. But from behind her came this strange whirling noise. Glancing back quickly, Mary Alice saw George coming up fast, riding a unicycle.

"How do you keep from falling over on that thing," Mary Alice asked the ghost as he sidled up next to her.

"Balance, it just takes balance," he cried with delight as he spread his arms and legs straight out. "Where did you get that nasty old riding contraption?"

"It was my mother's. I think she had this bike when she was a kid."

"You miss your mother, don't you?" George said.

"More than you will ever know"

"Oh yeah? Try me."

"What do you mean?" Mary Alice asked, squinting in the bright sunlight.

George put a frown on his face like he was thinking real hard. "I was such a shiftless youth," he said. "I was always hanging out in the saloons and pool parlors in my home town of Laurium."

"Where's Laurium?"

"In upper Michigan, on the shores of Lake Superior."

"So tell me about your mother?"

"Well, I was the youngest son in a family of eight. Both my parents had such high hopes for me. My dad would always criticize me, but my mother was always on my side; she would tell my dad, don't worry, he'll find out want he wants to do with his life soon enough."

They rode in silence for a while.

"Then I came to Notre Dame," George continued, "and my mother felt such pride that her wayward son was a college man."

"Then you should feel proud," Mary Alice said.

"Not really. I was just as shiftless at Notre Dame; I couldn't give up the card games and the pool parlors. I died before I could make it right with my mother. Still feel like I let her down."

"Maybe that's the reason why you cling to the Ghost World instead of going to Heaven." Mary Alice told him.

"You might be right."

"Your mother loves you; I'm sure she forgave you no matter how much you think you failed her," Mary Alice said. She was thinking of her own mother.

George went silent again, but by then they were in front of the Marian High School football field. The players on both sides were arriving in groups of twos and threes. They would be allowed to use the high school's gym locker room to dress for the game. Mary Alice would use, of course, the girl's locker room.

"You know," George said, "I never knew I could miss somebody so much, even after I have become a ghost."

"I guess we have something in common," Mary Alice agreed. "We both hope, somehow or some way, to see our mothers again."

Giving her that lopsided grin, George stopped his unicycle. "You got a big game today, Mary Alice. Win one for…oh…win the game for our mothers."

"I'll do my best…" but before she could say another word, George, and the unicycle, disappeared.

Mary Alice went directly to the girl's locker room, put the pads on, and was out on the field in no time flat. The Saint Stephen team was different in a strange sort of way; they were staring at her during warm-ups. Most of the guys on other teams would look the other way when she came near. Didn't want to acknowledge they would be playing against a girl. Well, the Saint Stephen's boy's stares didn't bug her at all. She knew it was intimidation on their part, an attempt to rattle her cage. It wouldn't work. She was getting excited about playing this game.

When the teams had finished their pregame warm-ups, both coaches met in the middle of the field. Bill Featherstone was the coach for Saint Stephen. He was a bull of a man, with a thick neck supported by powerful shoulders. "Hey coach," he bellowed at the equally large Coach Mike as they firmly shook hands. "Tell that big, bad girl of yours to take it easy on my poor little boys today. I wouldn't want to see any of my guys get hurt."

Coach Mike's full face turned a crimson red. Neither man moved. They glared at each other with their nostrils flaring. "Let's see how your ballerina boys match up against my big bad girl," Coach Mike said through gritted teeth. After that, he turned around and ran to rejoin his team, leaving Bill Featherstone standing by himself on the fifty-yard line.

Mary Alice was warming up her arm, throwing short passes to various players, when Coach Mike came up next to her. "What do you say?" he asked, placing both hands solidly on her shoulder pads. "Are you ready to play today?"

"Much more than that," Mary Alice said without hesitating. "I need to play today."

Coach Mike nodded; then a big smile spread across his face, something she had never seen him do before. "I feel sorry for those Saint Stephen boys." he said. "Just have a good time out there."

Did Coach tell her to have fun? She didn't know whether to laugh or cry but she was ready to go through a wall for Coach Mike if he wanted her to.

The bleachers were filling up nicely just as the two teams were lining up for the opening kickoff. Our Lady won the coin toss and elected to receive. Mary Alice, waiting on the sidelines for the first series of downs, scanned the bleachers. Nope, her dad wasn't there yet. Of course, he might be under the bleachers, gathering in bets on the game's outcome. Then she had a weird thought—was he betting that her team would win?

George was standing next to her where a moment before he wasn't. Startled, Mary Alice's eyes widened. "Why do you always have to show up that way?"

"What do you want me to do," George whined. "I'm a ghost, for crying out loud."

The kickoff was brought back to the thirty-five. Mary Alice dashed out to the huddle. Three plays later, Mary Alice was back on the sidelines. Our Lady stood at minus eight yards, the third down play a quarterback sack. Along the far sidelines, Bill Featherstone was slapping helmets and grabbing facemasks, screaming in his players' faces. In contrast, Coach Mike was off by himself, pacing up and down the sideline like a caged lion.

A minute later he was staring in disbelief. A Saint Stephen kid had just returned a punt for a touchdown. There was bedlam on the other side of the field, the fans going crazy, Bill Featherstone going crazy, the players bouncing around like Mexican Jumping beans.

George moved closer to Mary Alice, his eyes lighting up. "Say," he spoke softly, "if you like, I can use some ghost magic to help your team win this game."

"Don't even think about it," Mary Alice told him sternly. "We want to win this game fair and square."

Saint Stephen missed the extra point, and that made the Our Lady players feel a little better. Coming back from six was better than seven. Mary Alice peeked over at Coach Mike, to see how he was reacting to the returned punt. His stoic look made Mary Alice wonder, nobody really knows much about him. He was hired right before the first practice, coming from somewhere out of town. The sisters said he had fully experienced coaching credentials, how they found this out Mary Alice didn't know. He certainly was a mystery man.

Todd Hertel, on his way to the field for the kickoff, smacked Mary Alice on the back. "Okay, big shot quarterback," he taunted, "how about doing something for a change."

Mary Alice ignored him. Her focus was on the first play she would call on the next series of downs—forty-five cross buck.

Forty-five cross buck didn't gain a yard; neither did the next two plays. Our Lady punted again.

"Are you sure you don't want me to use some ghost magic?" George asked, popping up next to Mary Alice as she came off the field.

Starting to get a little irritated, she said, "George, aren't you supposed to be in the bleachers? Spectators aren't allowed to be on the field. If the coaches or refs see you down here, you will be thrown out of the stadium."

"That's just it," George replied, "nobody can see me right now but you, at least, I think so."

George turned to the player on his right side. "Can you see me kid?" he yelled. "Can you hear my voice?"

The player, Josh Cartwright, didn't flinch, didn't act like he heard or saw George.

"Yep," George said, "you are definitely the only one that knows I'm here. I can do that, you know, just be seen by those whom I want to see me."

"Well—go somewhere else, will ya," Mary Alice said, her voice rising.

"Sheesh—what a grouch!" George moved away all right, stalking down the sidelines, not around people, but through them as if they were not there.

"What do you mean go somewhere else?" Josh said to Mary Alice, looking at her strangely.

"I don't mean you, Josh. I was talking to…oh, never mind."

Mary Alice felt bad about being petty with George, but during a game her intensity level was raised to a fever pitch. When the whistle blew, she was all about the game, didn't want any kind of distraction.

Both sides spent the remaining minutes of the first half chasing first downs, the half ending with Saint Stephen still ahead six zip.

In the locker room, Coach Mike seemed to be disappointed, but he kept his cool, speaking to the players in an encouraging tone of voice, telling them to get plenty of water in them and get ready for a tough second half. On the other side, Bill Featherstone was going berserk. He was screaming, raving, acting loony and using really bad words. Everyone could hear him banging lockers, hopefully not with his player's heads. And his team was winning!

George was not visible when Mary Alice returned to the sidelines. She wanted to apologize for her rude behavior, but the second half began, and she was full bore back into the game.

The third quarter was more of the same. Our Lady stuffed Saint Stephen on their first possession, and after Our Lady received the punt on their own thirty-seven, the Saint Stephen fired-up wild bunch stopped them with a hustling, swarming defense. Bill Featherstone's crazy half-time shenanigans seemed to do the trick—his boys were ready to play.

This was good old-fashioned football with blitzes, end runs, quick openers, screen passes, even an occasional incomplete bomb. But no matter what the offenses tried throughout the second half, the defenses held their ground.

Finally, Our Lady had possession of the ball with 31 seconds left in the game, fourth down, sixty-three yards from pay dirt. Coach Mike called his last time out. He called Mary Alice and Todd over for a talk. "Okay you two, we're going to run the old fumblerooski. We have been practicing this play all season just for this kind of situation. Now, I know you two don't like each other, but we can win the game running this play if you two work together. Can I count on you?"

Mary Alice and Todd glared at each other and shook their heads yes. Coach wasn't sure about those two, but a bittersweet smile came to his face.

The teams lined up for the snap. The ball came up to Mary Alice's hands, but instead of snatching it, she kept her palms open so the ball would drop to the ground. She immediately made a bee-line down the field, running as fast as she could. At the same time, everyone along the line pulled out to their right like the play was going to be a power sweep. The defense followed suit, furiously fighting the lineman to get in the backfield. Todd, from his flanker position, held his ground—and then he scooped up the ball and went back to throw a pass. And who would be the receiver? Mary Alice!

There was a collective gasp from the fans in the bleachers. Mary Alice was wide open. The Saint Stephen players looked around, confused; they had no idea who had the ball. All Todd had to do was throw the dang football!

But he didn't—at first. "Throw the ball!" Mary Alice yelled. "Throw the ball!" Coach Mike yelled. Todd hesitated some more—then he heaved the football.

Mary Alice caught the football past midfield. She took off like a jackrabbit. The Saint Stephen players, alerted to what was happening, were in hot pursuit. Mary Alice got to the forty—the thirty—the twenty—she glanced to her left, noticing a presence—a would-be tackler? No, it was George, running along beside her. Could everyone see him? She hoped not. George was bounding along, waving his arms, and then suddenly he was on his unicycle, following Mary Alice across the goal line.

The game was tied! Mary Alice searched for George as she exchanged high-fives with her teammates—he was gone again. No time to wonder about that nutty ghost now, she was the kicker for the decisive extra point. Todd was the holder. The ball was snapped—Todd turned the laces away and got the ball down—Mary Alice swung her leg—her foot hit the ball—it soared—straight through the uprights. Our Lady was ahead by one with just enough time for the kickoff.

The Our Lady fans were ecstatic. They calmed down quickly as every pair of eyes concentrated on the upcoming kickoff. They had nothing to worry about. Saint Stephen tried the lateral play, with several hands touching the ball, but it was eventually fumbled out of bounds. Game over—Our Lady was the champion!

There is no greater feeling in sports than winning a championship. You are happy beyond your wildest dreams, knowing that you probably will never experience anything close to it again. So the Our Lady players and fans celebrated like it was New Year's Eve. They happily danced something resembling an Irish jig while pouring Cokes and Seven-Ups over each other's heads.

Everybody gathered in the middle of the field, to listen to Coach Mike. His eyes twinkled like a thousand stars. He cleared his hoarse throat. "I want to thank each and every one of you for the privilege to coach these fine young men—and one special young woman. You all worked hard throughout the season to get where we are now—champions of the ICCL!"

The crowd roared their approval, carrying on with their revelry. Coach Mike raised his big arms to shush them. "One more thing," he said. "Keep the pride you feel now for the rest of your lives. When things go bad for you, remember this joyful day, and you will persevere."

Later, at the Pizza Hut celebration party, Mary Alice noticed Coach Mike leave early. Where would he go? He didn't seem to have family in the area. She watched him walk out of the restaurant, pulling up the hood of his extra large sweatshirt against the rain that had begun to fall. There was something odd about this man, she just didn't know what it was.

She was more than glad George didn't grace her at the party with another embarrassing appearance. Nobody mentioned his exploits on the field when he ran with her for the game tying touchdown. Obviously, no one else saw him. But Halloween was two days away, and she, and others, would see him then.

## CHAPTER FOURTEEN

▼

The only thing certain about Halloween this year for Mary Alice was it would fall on October 31. How many living people, especially on the night of spooks and goblins, are allowed to enter a world solely inhabited by the spirits of the dead? First off, she promised Ricardo's mom she would take him trick or treating. Mary Alice felt she was too mature, now that she was thirteen, to put on a stupid costume and go around begging for candy, but she agreed to escort Ricardo from house to house for a couple of hours. Then she would go with George to the Notre Dame campus, to Washington Hall, and from there to the Ghost World.

Mary Alice told her dad she would spend the night with a friend, kind of an all night Halloween party. He seemed so preoccupied lately that he didn't even ask who the friend was, or where she lived, or anything about her. Leave it to her dad to be thinking only of himself. Why, he didn't even show up for the Pizza Hut celebration party after the game. Maybe there was more to it than she realized. Mary Alice noticed her dad was very pale lately, not eating at all well. He also trembled a lot, acted as if he was scared of something, but when Mary Alice would ask him about why he was so distressed—he would clam up and leave the room. Were the professional gamblers pressuring him to pay up what he owed them? Or was Sam Ridge somehow the cause of his anxiety. Her dad's lack of communication was the main reason why her mom had left home in the first place. It's really hard to help someone you love when they won't talk about what is bothering them. Chuck wasn't even calling her 'Kitten' anymore. Mary Alice never thought she would miss being called that childish name.

George made his usual otherworldly appearance by showing up out of thin air. He leaned toward Mary Alice and touched her hand. "Are you ready for the Ghost World?" he asked her tentatively.

To avoid meeting his eyes, Mary Alice kept her sight on the sidewalk. She was on her way to Ricardo's house. "I'm really scared, George," she said, her voice quivering." I know I gotta go to the Ghost World to save my dad, but I wish I didn't have to."

"Do you think it's gonna be any easier for me," George snapped, kicking a stone so hard that if he hadn't been a ghost the stone would have broken his foot. "I'll have to take you to the evil side of the Ghost World to find Sam Ridge's living crystal, and I don't mind telling you, I'm scared too."

Mary Alice's eyes narrowed, as she looked the ghost over long and hard. "I still can't get over that you guys can be scared."

"Maybe that's why we're ghosts. Maybe that's why we don't move on—we're just too afraid to face what is on the other side."

Concerned by the sharp edge in his voice, Mary Alice asked him, "How did you die anyway?"

An awkward silence passed between them. Finally George spoke in a slow, measured tone. "My death is the main reason why I am helping you with your dad. It was a cold rainy night in November and I was twenty-five years old. I was in Mishawaka, gambling as usual. A new pool parlor had opened that week. I never missed going to a new pool parlor because I would always make lots of money betting with reckless first time players. I would let them win a couple of games; then I would convince them to put all their money down on one more game, which I would win easily."

The sadness in George's voice almost brought Mary Alice to tears.

"I didn't stop there," George continued. "There was also a late night card game in a room upstairs. I won some and lost some, and by four o'clock in the morning I had had enough. By the time I got back to campus, after walking several miles in the rain, I was chilled to the bone. My dorm building was shut tight for the night. There was no way to get in so I went to sleep on the front steps of Washington Hall. Within a couple of days I was in the hospital with a high fever and a bad sore throat. I died soon after."

"I don't know what to say," Mary Alice said.

"Well I do," George told her boldly. "My gambling habit caused my death in a roundabout way. If my addiction to gambling hadn't got the better of me, I would have been back in my dorm room sleeping in a snug bed instead of walking around in the cold rain. Then, just maybe, I wouldn't have gotten sick. I could have lived a long productive life and made my parents proud."

George took a few deep breaths. "Anyway, that is why I want to help you with your dad. I know first handily what gambling can do to a person, how it can destroy a perfectly good life."

He waited for Mary Alice to say something. Finally she blurted out "thank s George."

"Maybe we can help each other," the ghost whispered.

They stopped in front of Ricardo's house. Ricardo must have been watching for Mary Alice because he came running out made up in a Zorro costume. His innocent smile sent a warm tremor rushing through her body.

"Hi" he said, facing Mary Alice. "Is…George… going…with…us?

"Yes, if you don't mind."

"Oh…I…don't…mind.      Where…is…your… costume…George?

Mary Alice couldn't help but laugh. If Ricardo only knew he was going trick-or-treating with a real ghost! "George doesn't have a costume," she finally said.

"Oh yes I do!" George shouted. There was suddenly a sheet spread over him, with holes for eyes and a mouth.

"How…did…you…do…that," Ricardo gasped, his eyes wide.

"He is just playing a Halloween trick on you," Mary Alice said before George could say anything else.

They went from house to house as the late afternoon sun fell away. Darkness came quickly, and with it a light north breeze that quickly lowered the temperature. Mary Alice was glad she wore a sweater.

As Ricardo bounded up to another house, Mary Alice and George waited at the sidewalk, as they had been doing all night. The night sky towered over them, bright stars visible between bare tree limbs.

"You sure are quiet," George said.

Mary Alice nodded. She was happiest when observing in silence, watching for small details; maybe be the one who would plan what would happen next.

After several more candy gathering stops, Ricardo was getting tired, starting to droop. They decided to go back to his house. A full moon had risen, looking much larger than it really was. All three stopped and gazed at the moon's glow, half excepting to see on the surface the image of a witch or a black cat. Thudding feet came up from behind them. A hand reached in and snatched Ricardo's trick or treat bag.

It took a little time to figure what was happening. George knew it first and didn't hesitate; he raised an arm. Three boys tumbled to the lawn, head over heels. The boys tried to get up but were stunned silly. George held them fast with his raised arm.

"Lemme up!" one boy yelled out. Mary Alice came close, and in the light from the full moon, she could clearly make out who he was. Todd Hertel.

"Todd, what are you doing? Did you steal Ricardo's trick or treat bag?"

"Not me! You didn't see me take anything!"

The trick or trick bag lay under a nearby tree, candy all over the place. Ricardo ran over and scooped up the bag, making sure all the candy was put back in.

"You can't prove I stole anything, Mary Alice," Todd sneered. "Just try to pin it on me. Go ahead, I dare ya."

Mary Alice groaned and shook her head. She was hoping, maybe too much, that the touchdown pass Todd threw to her in the championship game might change him for the better. Nope. Even after the game, there was no comradeship between them. He never came over to say nice catch, and she never had the chance to say nice throw. At the Pizza Hut celebration party, he kept his distance, leaving the party early to join his thug friends in some sort of mischief.

"Let him go," Mary Alice said to George, seeing the ghost's arm raised.

"Are you sure?"

"Yes, let him go."

George lowered his arm. Right way the boys were up and running, their dark clothing mixing in with the shadows of the night.

"I think you feel sorry for that boy," George told Mary Alice somberly.

"We have more important things to worry about," she replied.

Mary Alice remembered when Todd wasn't quite so nasty. There must be a reason he is now. She would give him the benefit of the doubt.

The ghost and the girl dropped Ricardo off at his house. Reluctantly, Mary Alice followed George down the lonely streets as most trick or treaters were done for the night. Nothing was said between them as they went down alleys and cut through back yards and open fields, eventually reaching the Notre Dame campus. Mary Alice would have liked nothing better than going home to her bed.

There was someone lurking behind them, hiding in the dark spots, keeping pace. This someone wanted to find out what Mary Alice and George were up to once and for all. If he could dig up some dirt about them, expose them for the devious characters they were, he could find a way to punish them for treating him with no respect.

Todd Hertel crouched behind the Administration Building's high front steps at the same time Mary Alice and George approached Washington Hall. He watched them keenly as they went inside. He had them now! Trespassing on private property. All he had to do was wait a while before following them in, and if he were lucky, maybe he would see them steal something. Then he could go to the cops and get them in all kinds of trouble.

## CHAPTER FIFTEEN

▼

The Washington Hall lobby was pitch-black except for a faint night-light stuck in a wall socket. Mary Alice brought along a regular flashlight, so she flicked it on. She didn't want to turn on the ceiling fluorescent lights because that would have caused unwanted attention from anyone passing by.

George glided past Mary Alice, but before he could completely get by, she grabbed his arm. She pointed the flashlight beam to a window high on a far wall. The faint image of a head moved against the muted light. "Do you see that head?" Mary Alice asked barely above a whisper. There was no real reason to talk that way; it just seemed the right thing to do.

"Oh yea," George said.

"Do you know what it is?"

"A ghost, no doubt," he replied as a matter of fact.

"Are there more ghosts here than you?"

"Well, sure. An old building such as this one holds a lot of ghosts."

"But all I see is a reflection. Do ghosts have reflections?"

"Mary Alice, ghosts are the reflections of departed souls."

A trumpet's dulcet tones filled the lobby. Mary Alice could feel an icy invisible presence. She took several small steps backwards.

"Oh the trumpet playing; you're probably wondering about that," George said. "It's coming from the ghost of a student trumpeter who died about the same time I did. He's just saying hello."

"How about telling him goodbye, "Mary Alice said irritably.

"I believe he is playing a perfect B flat," George said. "Don't worry, he will move on soon."

The trumpet sound faded away. Mary Alice wondered if there were other ghosts inside the walls, watching their every movement. That was an unsettling thought.

They came to the top of a stairway that led to the basement. There was a light switch on the nearby wall. George pulled it up with a finger—and there was light over the steps. Mary Alice's face had turned into an unhealthy shade of ghastly green. Her stomach felt as if it was being punctured by needles. "Are you scared, George?" she asked, her voice trailing away.

"In this building, no, this is home to me."

"Well, I'll tell you what," Mary Alice said, sweeping unruly hair from her face, "I'll be scared for the both of us."

"That works for me. C'mon, let's go downstairs."

A pair of sneaky eyes watched them make their descent. Todd Hertel had opened the front door ever so slightly, squeezing through without making a sound. He stayed in a dingy corner until Mary Alice and George moved to the stairs, then, when he could see them going down, he came after them.

There was a metal door at the foot of the stairs that George easily opened with ghostly magic. Mary Alice again clicked on her flashlight. Going inside a room, she spread illumination around—stopping when she came upon a large mass of twisted metal, with pipes leading in many different directions. It didn't take very long to figure out this was a heating system, a furnace, the main heating source for the entire building.

"We gotta crawl in that thing," George said out of the side of his mouth. He went over to a wall and switched on the overhead lights.

"What!" Mary Alice could not believe what she was hearing. "It has to be filthy in that furnace. Are you sure?"

George's eyes darted from side to side. "That furnace is our portal to the Ghost World," he said, moving forward. "It's the only way down there."

"I don't know about this…wait, what do you mean by down?"

"Don't think about it. Just grab my hands and let's go."

True to his word, George reached for Mary Alice and pulled her into a man-sized pipe. Down they went—head first.

At the metal door, Todd watched the ghost and the girl, leaning flat against a wall to make sure he was not seen. To his astonishment, he saw them dive into the furnace pipe. It almost seemed the furnace had swallowed them whole. He ran over and peered into the pipe. It was too dark to see anything. Well, if they could dive in, so could he. But he wouldn't go in head first—no way—so he climbed on top of the pipe and lay down on his back, hanging on to the pipe's edge. Letting go, he went down like he was on a playground slide.

Mary Alice pressed close behind George without feeling him. She was moving down the pipe at breath taking speed, a runaway human rollercoaster. Whooshing airflow pounded her eyeballs and pierced her eardrums. The whole world was turning upside down and Mary Alice was along for the ride.

She landed on her stomach. The first thing she saw was George standing with his arms folded as if he had been waiting for her for long time. The ghost was glowing, dazzling in a yellow hue. Mary Alice tried to steady her breathing. Squinting, she fought the urge to close her eyes.

"Oh boy," George told her, "I'm too bright, aren't I." Holding on to his nose, George turned in circles, and the more he turned, the less bright he became. "Sorry about that. In the Ghost World we ghosts become as brilliant as the sun if we don't turn it down. It just happens."

"I'm sure!" Mary Alice got to her feet and steadied herself. She glanced suspiciously at four white walls. "Where are we?"

"I guess you could call this room the vestibule to the Ghost World," George said. "From here we will have to find our way to the underworld. But first, let me show you something."

A clunky whirling sound came from the far wall. The noise abruptly stopped as a massive door twenty feet high suddenly appeared. The door opened without a sound. George beckoned Mary Alice to follow him. The door closed behind them, vanishing from sight.

They entered a great hall that seemed to stretch forever. Shelves higher than they could see lined the walls. On the shelves were clear crystals stacked neatly together, so close they looked like rows of polished silver sandstones.

"These," George said, sweeping an arm, "are the living crystals of everyone who has ever lived a good life."

Mary Alice breathed out loud. "Oh wow! But where are the crystals of those who are evil?"

George frowned. "They are in the underworld. And, sorry to say, that is where we have to go if we want to find Sam Ridge's living crystal."

Back in the white room, Todd coasted to a stop flat on his back. He wanted to stand but his legs were too wobbly. The ride down the pipe caused him to become a little light headed. He wiped the sweat from above his forehead against an arm of his long sleeve shirt. As he looked around, the white room seemed to grow smaller.

His breath came in short spurts. "Anybody here?" he shouted. There was a hum coming through the walls, sounding like spoken words that were impossible to make out. "Is there anybody here?"

There was no answer, or least none that he could understand. He didn't know what frightened him more, the disturbing voices or the shrinking room. Maybe following Mary Alice and George down here wasn't such a good idea. Where were they any way?

The ghost and the girl were making their way through the great hall of the living crystals. Mary Alice rubbed her hands together. The white light of the hall made her cheeks look almost transparent. "George, I hate to ask you this," she finally blurted out, "but how do we get to the underworld?"

"That's a good question," George mused, rubbing his chin. "Never been there before."

Mary Alice put a hand over her mouth and pulled in a hard, mucous filled pant. "What is that?" she said, pointing to a nearby wall. In bold black letters, words were appearing in very neat print. It seemed as if someone invisible was painstakingly typing the words on the wall.

**HELLO MY DEARS.THIS IS YOUR OLD PAL JACK BUMBLEBEE.**

George looked at Mary Alice and shrugged.

**YOU CAN TALK TO ME. I CAN HEAR YOU.**

"Uh," Mary Alice said tentatively, "we were just wondering—how do we get to the underworld?"

**ALL RIGHT YOUNG LADY; THAT IS WHY I AM, SO TO SPEAK, WRITING TO YOU. YOU MUST KEEP GOING UNTIL YOU COME TO A RUSTY METAL DOOR. THE DOOR WILL OPEN WHEN YOU RAP IT TWICE. GO INSIDE, AND THERE YOU WILL COME ACROSS A LARGE GONDOLA SECURED WITH ROPE. GET INSIDE THE GONDOLA AND LOWER YOURSELFS, USING THE ROPE AS A FULCRUM. WHEN YOU REACH THE BOTTOM, YOU WILL BE IN THE UNDERWORLD. AND BE CAREFUL.**

Mary Alice wiped her snot filled nose with a sleeve of her sweater. "Be careful of what?"

**I GOT TO GO NOW. GOOD LUCK WITH YOUR QUEST. YOUR SINCERE FRIEND, JACK BUMBLEBEE**

"What do you think he means—be careful?" Mary Alice asked George.

George gave her a sick grin—then turned his attention further down the hall. "I don't know, but we had better be ready for anything," he said. "I will say one thing about Jack, he sure does write a nice letter."

Shaking her head, Mary Alice went with George, looking for the metal door. The sad part was, she hoped they wouldn't find it.

Todd was also in the hall of the living crystals. His dizziness had passed so he was on his feet. The massive door had appeared and opened again, and not knowing what else to do, he went into the great hall. He was wondering what the rows and rows of shelves were holding. Clear, round shaped objects. It didn't make sense, but then, nothing about Mary Alice and George made sense. He decided to keep going, hoping to find them, or maybe find a way out of this bad dream.

The ghost and the girl also kept going, looking for any kind of a door that seemed even a little bit corrosive. George bounded nearly to the top of the shelves every now and then, to see farther away, but still no metal door.

"Could we rest a minute?" Mary Alice asked, and not waiting for George's answer, she flopped down onto the clean marble floor. She closed her eyes. It would be so easy to go to sleep here, with nobody to bother her. Nobody live anyway.

A brown piece of metal hit the top of her head. Mary Alice brushed it away. Then another piece hit her. She cocked an eye and looked up. More metal was falling, coming down like metallic rain. She leaped to her feet and pointed up. "There it is George!"

The ghost looked up and groaned. "I see it!"

And there, on a high vaulted ceiling, was a big old metal door.

He soared straight up before Mary Alice could make another move. The heavy metal door was brown with flaking rust. "Remember what Jack said," Mary Alice yelled through cupped hands. "Knock two times."

George knocked—nothing happened. He rapped his knuckles two more times. Still nothing. He was wondering what else he could do when the door opened with a rush.

A wind came out of the opening, violent, cyclonic, drawing Mary Alice straight up. She tried to grab hold of the door with one hand, no use—she went spiraling through the open vortex. George, powerless to help her, watched her sail by. He dove in after her.

They spun with the wind. Mary Alice screamed, but the sound was swallowed by the roaring tempest. Long, thin wisps came into view; the wisps resembled people with the crazed look of the eternally lost. They tumbled with Mary Alice and George, staring at them with hideous, empty eyes.

The ghost and the girl landed with a jolt on jagged ground. Dazed, Mary Alice touched the surface just to be sure it was solid and real. Yep, the ground felt hot and rock hard. At least the scary wisps had disappeared, though she felt their invisible hands running across her flesh. She shook and couldn't feel them anymore. "Is this the underworld?" she asked George.

"Yeah, I guess so," he said grimly, looking up at the open door in the red sky. He was glad to see the door still open.

George didn't like being down here, he wasn't positive he could get them back through that door. The best thing to do was keep Mary Alice convinced he knew what he was doing. Hopefully, the pain and misery of this wretched place wouldn't show its ugly face.

Todd Hertel was starting to feel real panic. He saw an open, rusty door in the ceiling. What was that for? Suddenly he was head over heels. He tried to scream, but you need air to scream, and he couldn't find any in the swirling winds that had pulled him through the opening. All he could do was close his eyes and wish himself away.

He landed in a crater. Two figures were running towards him, but as he squinted into a steaming mist, he couldn't bring them into focus. Scrambling to his feet, he looked around, hoping to find of a place to run. There was nothing there but hot steam coming out of more craters. He turned and peered at the figures again. They were becoming clear.

"It's Todd Hertel!" Mary Alice shouted at George.

Todd staggered backward. "Get me out of here!"

"What are you doing here anyway?" Mary Alice asked him as she stuck a finger in his chest.

"I…wanted to see what you guys were up to."

"If I told you why we are here, you wouldn't believe it," Mary Alice said. But Mary Alice told him about Sam Ridge's living crystal anyway, and how they had to find the crystal to save her dad. She also told him all about Jack Bumblebee and that George is a real live, or dead, ghost. Todd had a look of disbelieve, but his face lit up when Mary Alice told him about Sam Ridge's disguise, the hooded sweatshirt.

"I… saw him!" he stammered. "I saw him at Pinhook Park. Somehow he made me come close to him, and I felt his breath draw something out of me."

"He was drawing fear out of you, to make himself stronger," George told him. "He is after you too. Now, I don't see where you have a choice, but will you agree to help us?"

"Yeah," Todd admitted, "I see what you mean. What can I do to help you guys find this Sam Ridge's crystal?"

"First off," Mary Alice said, "did you come down here in a gondola?"

"A gondola, what's that? No, a big wind pulled me through a door or a hole in the roof or something. I went around in circles and ended inside a crater. What's this about a gondola?"

"Jack Bumblebee told us a gondola would bring us down here," George said. "He probably made it up, knowing we would not want to get caught in that whirlwind like we were. If we had known, we might have figured the best thing to do would be to forget about coming to this desolate place."

"Isn't Jack Bumblebee the old crazy janitor at our school?"

"Yes, but he is not as he appears. I wonder if we can trust him."

Mary Alice bit her lower lip. "Let's just hope he really is on our side."

Todd went with the ghost and the girl, but he wasn't happy about it. He watched for any means of escape. If he could get away without his new allies, well, so much the better.

A piece of burning ember hit Todd in the middle of his back. He looked up to see ash falling from the sky. Feeling real terror, he whirled around, looking for a place to run.

"This way," George called out as he sprinted toward a gap in the ground. All three reached the gap at the same time. They skidded to a stop, crouching on all fours, their heads tucked under their bodies. Hot ash kept falling—a firestorm. Any exposed skin was stung with small pellets of fire.

"What's going on," Todd whined, keeping his head down. Just then the fiery shower stopped completely.

George flew to the top of the gap, and then leaped to the greater rise of a clump of rocks. "Come up here and take a look," he shouted.

Mary Alice and Todd crawled to rock's highest point. They saw a vast inferno lake. Hot blasts of air were blowing off the lake, making breathing a little more difficult. "So that was where the burning embers were coming from," Mary Alice said.

The ghost nodded. The fiery conditions didn't seem to bother him as much as the other two. "You're not going to like this," George said, trying to smile, "but I think we have to cross that fire lake to find Sam Ridge's living crystal."

"How are we going to do that?" Todd asked, looking around. "I mean, we can't swim in fire. Well, maybe you can, being a ghost and all, but we sure can't"

"I don't know," George said uncertainly. "We'll go down to the shore, and hope to find a way over."

Mary Alice remained quiet. She was trying to be brave, trying not to lose hope. Only her trust in George kept her going. And she knew she would not go home without the living crystal of Sam Ridge.

They stumbled down to the shore and paused, wondering what to do next. Then they saw a strange sight. A bizarre creature approached them, walking on four legs, half animal and half man. The creature had the upper torso of a Roman centurion, with a plumed bronze helmet and highly shined breastplate armor. But attached to the armor, most amazedly, were miniature human heads acting as ringbolts, some with expressions of utter sorrow, others with looks of confusion, still others with the demented look of the insane. Beneath this strange armor were the four legs of an animal, perhaps a large wolf, or a bear.

"Hello, I don't receive many guests here," the creature said in a most cordial manner as he came to a standstill. Julius Caesar is my name. What might be the reason you have come to visit me this fine day."

George nudged Mary Alice, to prod her to talk. Err... are you the Julius Caesar of the history books?" she asked stiffly.

"Well, I was a Roman dictator, if that is what you mean. Now, what do you want from me."

"We need to find a way to cross this lake of fire," she told him. Mary Alice didn't think it prudent under the circumstances to ask Julius how he ended up with the four legs of an animal.

"And why would you want to cross my beautiful lake?"

Mary Alice couldn't help but stare at the human head ringbolts. A few were now horribly weeping while others were laughing hysterically. It was very unnerving. Still, she had to keep talking. "We are seeking the living crystals of the evil." Not trusting this strange creature, she did not mention anything about Sam Ridge.

Julius thought for a minute and then smiled broadly. "I will take you all across, think no more about it."

Todd screwed up his face. "And how do you figure on doing that?" he asked like a real snot.

"Why, my water boat, my fine young friend," Julius said, and he turned around on all fours and pointed with a paw at the burning lake. There, bobbing in the fiery flames was a boat that looked to be put together with pulsating water.

They all hurried down to the shoreline. The water boat was a queer vessel indeed. On all sides were quivering masses of water that were somehow held together to form a craft about the size of a life boat.

"Step lively now," Julius merrily said. He extended a paw towards Mary Alice, to help her into the boat. She blushed, not used to courteous manners. Stepping carefully, afraid she would fall through the watery deck— she went aboard. But when her feet hit the water, she stayed firm, not sinking at all. The others followed her into the boat, with Julius getting on last.

"Okay Julius," Todd said, "how does this boat sail?"

"Allow me to show you. But I have to tell you, young man, you ask way too many questions." Julius went to the back of the boat and squatted down. The boat began moving, the flames parting, slowly at first, but then rapidly. And what was the means of propulsion? Why, it was Julius' bushy tail which was turning like a propeller.

Calming down for the first time in a long while, Mary Alice settled back and closed her eyes. Then, without a glint of warning, she felt a strange rocking sensation coming from under the boat. She looked up with horror as two giant heads broke through the flaming surface next to her, followed by two long slender necks attached to a wale shaped body. On both sides of the animal, where arms or legs or even fins should be, were tiny wings, way too small for an animal that size. In spite of all that, the animal took flight, directly over the water boat.

Everybody on board dove to the bottom of the boat, everybody, that is, but Julius. "Now don't tell me you all are afraid," he said, actually looking surprised. "Allow me to introduce you to my good friend Augustus."

Augustus glided down to the boat, peering at those inside with four coal black eyes. Julius reached out and began to caress one of the animal's bony beaks. Augustus let out a guttural meow—much deeper than a cat but the same meow.

George was the first to look up, and the others soon followed. "What kind of critter is that?" He asked Julius.

"Augustus is what I call an anfibird—a combination of an animal, a fish, and a bird." Julius said. "He will guide us across the lake. All we have to do is follow him."

George looked open-mouthed at Mary Alice who looked strangely at Todd who expectantly looked like he was going to cry.

The water boat trailed behind Augustus for another half-hour. Mary Alice saw it first, but soon all aboard were able to take a gander at a mammoth jetty thrusting out of the lake of fire. The jetty was shaped like a rocky skull. Clearly visible, in the eye sockets of the skull, were two cavernous caves.

"Stop here," George ordered. He casually moved over to Mary Alice. "I believe this is where we will find the living crystals," he told her in a low voice.

Julius beached the boat on the shoreline rocks while Augustus settled down on top of the rocky skull. There was no wind, just eerie quiet. Todd jumped out of the boat and slid to the rocky surface. "Ouch!" he cried, rubbing his shin. "That hurt. I don't like this place. I want to go home."

Mary Alice blew up. "Nobody asked you to follow us here, so shut up!" Turning her attention to George, and pointing to the eye socket caves, she asked, "Do you think the crystals might be inside."

"I can fly up there to find out for sure," George said, "but there is no way up for you mortals. The jetty's much too smooth and slick, plus there is nothing to grab hold for climbing. Maybe I can find Sam Ridge's crystal by myself."

"Ah, I know a way," Julius said as he looked directly up the jetty at the anfibird. "Augustus, my friend, might you indulge us by coming down here."

Augustus plopped down on the hard shoreline, meowing contently.

"Stretch your necks up to the caves, if you please," Julius instructed politely. "And keep as still as you can."

The anfibird gave him longing looks and immediately raised his two necks and heads, one to each eye socket cave.

"Now just climb up one of his nice scaly necks," Julius told everybody.

Mary Alice half-heartily set one of her tennies on one of Augustus' necks and warily began to climb. The neck was scaly all right, but the scales made it easy for her to go up hand over hand due to the hold on nature of its surface. Gaining confidence as she climbed higher, Mary Alice was soon at the level of the caves. She stepped off Augustus' head with aplomb. She found out one thing real quick: It was hot up there!

Wiping the sweat from her forehead with a hanky, Mary Alice hollered down, "Todd, are you coming up?"

Todd held the expression of one who has no idea what he wants to do. There was no way he wanted to clamber up one of the monster's necks, and he especially didn't want to be anywhere near one of its heads.

"Boy, you can stay down here with me, "Julius told him with a gleam in his eye. "We can keep each other company—won't that be fun?"

That was all Todd needed to hear. He scaled up one of Augustus' necks faster than a mountain lion. George, chuckling, flew up and met Mary Alice and Todd in front of the eye sockets caves.

Mary Alice trained her eyes down on Julius and the water boat. Lounging against one of the rocks, Julius seemed contented. "You don't think he will leave us here," Mary Alice said with a hint of fear.

"I sure hope not," George said. "C'mon, let's go inside one of the caves. The sooner we can find Sam Ridge's crystal, the sooner we can get out of this place."

It turned out that both of the skull's eye sockets emptied into a one large cave. There were no cracks in the walls or anything resembling a window to let light in, so Mary Alice unhooked the flashlight from her belt. She swept the opened flashlight around the cave. Against a moss covered wall were cages constructed out of bones.

And inside each cage were dark colored crystals, dark because these were the living crystals of the evil.

"We found them!" Mary Alice called out. But she immediately quieted down. "Where do we start to find Sam Ridge's crystal?"

"I don't know," George said. "I guess we will just have to get lucky."

They were not alone in the room. Something was flying overhead, something long and sleek.

Todd peered through the murky darkness. "What do you think it is," he asked George as he backed heavily into one of the cages. The cage was shattered. One of the crystals tumbled out, rolling out of the cave. Mary Alice ran after it, snatching the crystal before it could drop off the edge of the jetty.

Whatever was flying overhead was forgotten when the boys heard Mary Alice squeal. They ran to her side as fast as they could.

"I think this is It!" she cried.

George took the crystal from out of her hands and inspected it closely. Under a layer of dirt was part of an inscription. The word—Ridge—was faintly visible. "Let me have your handkerchief," George said to Mary Alice. After cleaning off most of the dirt, George tilted the crystal to read the rest of the engraving.

"This is it all right," he said. Mary Alice and Todd leaned in closer to get a better look. Sam Ridge's name was clearly etched in the crystal.

"Then let's get out of here!" Todd yelled. He immediately slid down on one of Augustus' two necks, not a smart thing to do on a scaly surface. He was soon doubled over in obvious pain.

The ghost and the girl tried not to laugh as they climbed down. Then again, they were jubilant with the success of their search.

The journey back to the original shoreline went a lot faster because Julius fastened Augustus with cable he found at the foot of the cave. It was a simple matter of Augustus pulling them back, swimming through the blazing waves with power and grace.

"I hope your trip was rewarding," Julius told the young people as he unleashed Augustus from the cable. Augustus rose to the red sky, and after doing a couple of flyovers, he blasted out a thundering meow of a goodbye and flew off, quickly disappearing over the horizon.

After they all bid Julius Caesar a happy farewell, George led the other two back to the rusty door they had originally been blown through. Mary Alice clutched Sam Ridge's living crystal with firm fingers. She wasn't about to let go of it now.

A large gondola was there, seemingly waiting for their arrival. The gondola was attached with a pulley and rope to the still open metal door. The swirling wind was gone.

"Hey, that's the gondola Jack Bumblebee told us about," George said. "You two get in, I'll pull you up."

Mary Alice climbed in right away but Todd wasn't so sure. He hesitated, then took a deep breath and practically crawled inside. His damp hand slid on top of the sidewall and he hooked his fingers and held tight.

Levitating to the top of the gondola, George pulled on the rope. He stopped for a second to steady his grip, and then he heaved mightily. The gondola was moving up slow but sure.

Todd made a big effort to remain calm, but the thing he didn't want to tell the others was he was extremely afraid of heights. That was the reason he got off from the skull cave so quickly, he was feeling shaky. But now, as he flexed his arms and legs and ordered himself to relax, he felt he would be all right. And he would have been if they hadn't been attacked by three of the flying serpents. George saw them first and yelled, "Duck your heads!" The serpents were coming in fast, like dive-bombers. Mary Alice got down right away but Todd wasn't so lucky. One of the serpents caught Todd's shirtsleeve in it fangs and began to jerk. Screaming, Todd lost his grip on the sidewall. He was savagely being taking away from the gondola.

George couldn't take his hands off the rope for fear the gondola would crash. There was nothing he could do to save Todd from his terrible fate.

A hand reached up and grabbed Todd's left foot. Mary Alice was holding on for all she was worth. It became a tug of war, with Mary Alice getting a hold on Todd's shin. Back and forth they went. Finally, Todd's shirt ripped, hurtling him and Mary Alice to the bottom of the gondola. At the same time, George pulled the gondola through the door. The gondola landed with a thud on the marble floor. The door closed tight with none of the serpents making it inside.

They sat there panting, waiting for their hearts to stop beating so fast. Todd looked at Mary Alice with surprise. "You…saved… my life," he said between forced breaths.

"Well, of course I did, I couldn't let one of those mean old freaks take you away."

"Thank…thank…you," Todd said with great difficulty.

There was no reason to remain in the great hall, so George immediately guided them back to the vestibule of the Ghost World. They coasted back through the furnace pipe, landing in the basement of Washington Hall.

As they tiredly trekked up the steps to return to the lobby, Mary Alice still held tight to Sam Ridge's living crystal. "I wonder how we are going to trap Sam Ridge in this thing," she said to George.

The ghost looked pensive. "Well, if Todd will help us, I have a plan."

## CHAPTER SIXTEEN

▼

Maybe for the first time in his life, Todd Hertel felt good about himself. He was now Tough Todd Hertel, the nemesis of all that is evil. His alliance with Mary Alice and George made him feel like he belonged, made him feel like he was part of a caring family. Home, the one with his mom and dad, well, there was no comparison. Dad was still the dictator of Planet Hertel and mom still didn't care. Mary Alice and George were his brother and sister in arms, kindred spirits in the battle against the wicked forces of the underworld. Bring 'em on!

He was riding his red Schwinn down Bittersweet Road, having just left his uncle's Granger farm. He had spent the day, a Saturday, helping his uncle with the last of the year's fall corn harvest. Farming was something Todd thought he would like to do when he was a grown man. Purdue has a great agricultural school, so when he graduates from there in the not so distant future, he will buy his own farm and show the world the best way to grow things.

All was well in his mind when the battered old pickup truck forced him off the road. He was just going over a small hill when he saw the truck barreling down on him, going much too fast for this two lane road. Todd waved at the driver, trying to get his attention, but the speed of the truck actually increased. Not having time to think about it—Todd veered his bike past the outer edge of the truck's hanging rear bumper.

Immediately Todd's bike shot off the road, but he could still feel the air stream coming off the back of the truck. He was headed for a cornfield.

Todd gripped the handlebar and brakes, his face turning away from the brittle stalks so his face would not get cut. He gripped the brakes too hard—so they locked, and since he was going downhill, he lost all control. Finally the front wheel hit a twisted vine, slowing him down enough so he could stop.

He wasn't hurt; he was sure about that. And the bike seemed to be okay, no dents or flat tires or broken chains or anything like that. He looked around—nothing to see but rows and rows of crusty yellowed stalks, the corn they once supported long harvested.

Todd breathed in deeply, wishing to find a way out of this maze of stalks. A strange feeling came over him, a feeling of not knowing where he was. This strange feeling was quickly turning into panic. His heart began to hammer and he started to sweat even though this was a cool day. Fear was coming back into his life.

Was he being watched? He had the sudden and illogical fear the stalks were monitoring his every move, waiting for a chance to strike. It seemed as though shadowy monsters armed with sharp knives were surrounding him.

The shakes shuddered through him. He licked his lips, got back on his bike and started to pedal slowly, hoping the road was not far away.

But he was becoming more lost.

Riding his bike up and down the rows of stalks, Todd could not find a way out. He hopped off the bike in a clearing and sat down with his head between his legs, sobbing hopelessly. A solitary scarecrow was stuck up behind his back. The scarecrow's head was a tilted jack-o'-lantern that was falling into decay with worms crawling through its withering eyes, nose, and mouth.

The sky began to darken, another disturbing night ahead. Todd could hear it, faint at first, the sound of something moving through the stalks. The sound came closer, turning into heavy feet crunching and crackling on the dried corn leaves. And there he was, standing over him, the hooded figure –Sam Ridge.

"What are you crying about boy?" Sam Ridge hissed through the deep black hood he always wore. "Are you afraid of me?"

Todd tried not to cower too much. "Please don't hurt me," he begged, his voice shaking. He felt a profound urge to run away and hide—but where could he go? So despite his fears, he slowly rose to meet Sam Ridge head-on. Todd was getting closer—he took something out from under his jacket, something dim but smooth, the living crystal—he shoved the crystal inside Sam Ridge's hood—he listened to him scream. Sam Ridge saw his face reflected in the murky glass! He began to narrow and shrink as he was drawn in, first his head, then his chest and stomach, eventually his legs. The evil Sam Ridge was a prisoner inside the crystal.

Yelling a victory whoop, Todd held the crystal high over his head. Just then, Mary Alice and George emerged from behind the stalks they were hiding behind and joined Todd in his celebration.

"Your plan worked perfectly," Todd told George excitedly. "Using me as a decoy—brilliant!"

"Thanks, but all the credit goes to you for carrying out the plan so well. I figured he would be trailing you, wanting to feed off more of your fear. All we had to do was get him in an out of the way place and he would be ours. When you stuck the crystal in his hood, he had to see his reflection, so he was trapped."

Todd gave Mary Alice a friendly jab on the shoulder. "Tell your cousin he came too close to me with his truck," he said, trying to keep a straight face. "That was almost too real."

"He just got his license yesterday," she said in turn trying to sound insulted. But her voice rang hallow. "You're lucky he didn't really hit you." They both began to laugh.

Holding the crystal out for all to see, Todd took great pride in his accomplishment, feeling like a conquering hero. Inside the murky crystal, a miniature Sam Ridge floundered about, pressing his arms and hands against the inner surface, the hood still hiding his face.

"Let's get the crystal to Jack Bumblebee right away," Mary Alice said, breaking the levity by sounding serious. The others became silent. They all knew there was more to be done before Sam Ridge could be destroyed forever.

## CHAPTER SEVENTEEN

Mary Alice's cousin dropped them off in front of Jack Bumblebee's house forty-five minutes later. The beige bungalow house seemed a little different. A row of squared–off bushes lined the front of the house, and the lawn was neatly trimmed, compared to the last time Mary Alice and George were here when the lawn was filled with dandelion weeds.

After telling her cousin they could get home on their own, Todd removed his bike from the back of the truck. Mary Alice led the two boys to the front door—which was already open. They went inside on the sly, a little skittish, unsure just what they would run into. The hallway also wasn't the same; it was shorter and well lighted and not at all forbidding. There was no need for a flashlight but George still had to be held down so he wouldn't float away.

They did not have to go far very far before they saw the red light, and under the light, jovial and fat as ever, sat Jack Bumblebee on a silver throne. "Greetings, my dears," he said in a booming voice. "Do you have some good news for me?"

Mary Alice licked her dry lips before speaking. "We have captured Sam Ridge," she said with a stout-heart. She held up the crystal with the murderer imprisoned inside. "We have done as you asked."

"Wonderful, my dears. Now let me have the crystal."

"I will be glad to get rid of this," Mary Alice said. She approached Jack and handed him the crystal. "What are you going to do with Sam Ridge?"

Jack Bumblebee laughed long and hard. "Oh, I have a great idea what to do with him," he managed to say between guffaws. "Would you all like to see?"

They all nodded enthusiastically. Jack Bumblebee stood and raised the crystal high over his head, his eyes twinkling like neon lights. He raised it even higher, on the tip of his fingers, and cried out," Come to me, master!" Then he flung the crystal to the floor.

The three kids looked on in horror as the crystal shattered into a thousand little pieces. There, smack down on the floor, was the tiny hooded Sam Ridge, and then he began to shoot up until he was normal size again. He stood defiantly before them with his arms clasped behind his back.

"Master, I have done as you asked," Jack Bumblebee proudly said. And then Jack's total appearance changed— he turned into the repulsive, bony shape of the school janitor. He kneeled down and bowed in front of Sam Ridge, spreading his hands on the floor.

"You have done well, Bumblebee," Sam Ridge told him. "You shall be rewarded. Now rise to your feet, we must deal with our guests."

Mary Alice could not believe what was happening. Was this all a nightmare? No, this was real because Sam Ridge was standing right in front of her, and he was speaking.

"Bumblebee my good friend, secure the boys, if you please."

"Yes master, right away master," Jack Bumblebee answered with great cheer. He pulled out a wand from under his janitor shirt and waved the wand over George and Todd. Instantly the boys were bound against a wall with chains, arms and legs no longer free. George looked really angry, but Todd once again looked really scared.

Bumblebee paused, and looked at Sam Ridge with a tilted head. "And what about the girl?"

"Ah, I know just what to do with her," Sam said bitterly.

He walked over to the terrified girl and placed a hand under her chin, lifting her face. With his other hand Sam reached for his hood, and in one complete swoop pulled it back. Mary Alice stared at his face with wide eyes. Round cheeks and a crooked nose—the face under the hood was that of Coach Mike!

Coach Mike—or rather Sam Ridge--leaned back his head and laughed loudly. "So now girl, you know my secret. Your coach turns out to be your enemy. That is so sad."

Shocked, Mary Alice slumped down on the floor. "What...what do you want from us?" she stammered, her voice well below freezing.

"I just want something from you. I want you to bring your father to me—tonight."

The defeated girl sat motionless, her eyes brimming with tears.

"Now don't cry," Sam told her, swishing a finger in front of her face. "Remember, you are a quarterback, and quarterbacks don't ever cry."

He circled around her, quiet for a while, but then he spoke. "I need your father to fulfill my destiny, to achieve my rightful place as lord over this mortal world. Now go and bring him to me. Tell your dad Coach Mike needs to see him immediately."

"What if I don't," Mary Alice gasped.

Sam Ridge moved over to the two boys still entangled in chains. "If you want to see them again," he said spitefully, "you will do as I command." Without another word Sam grasped Todd's head with both hands and blew in his nose. Todd's chin dropped to his chest.

"Oh look," Sam Ridge said as he turned around to face Mary Alice, "Todd seems to be a little under the weather. If you don't want his sickness to be permanent, you will bring your father to me."

Mary Alice quickly got to her feet and darted for the front door. The sound of Sam Ridge's sinister laugh kept repeating in her brain cells as she exited the house. She hopped on Todd's bike, pedaling furiously, trying to get that horrid laughter out of her head. Keeping her eyes steadily on the road, she continued to pump the pedals like she was a piston machine, her face grim and sure. She knew just where to find her dad on a Saturday night—Hullie and Mike's poolroom.

She kept thinking about Coach Mike, or Sam Ridge. She knows he feeds off the fear of the lost and hopeless, so that was why he came to town in the guise of a coach—it was the best way to get close to her and her gambling addicted dad. The goodhearted nuns at school probably hired him as coach of the football team to give him a break; he had the appearance of a man down on his luck. And that was the same reason the nuns had hired Jack Bumblebee as a janitor. Evil always takes advantage of all that is good in this world. But to save George and Todd, she would have to bring her dad back to the Bumblebee house, even though she knows Sam Ridge will use his fear to become immortal. Then Sam would have enough strength to cause pain and destruction to thousands of innocent people throughout the world. She started to cry again. What should she do?

Hullie and Mike's poolroom was crowded, with half-drunk men and painted women milling about inside, and a few lounging outside smoking cigarettes. Mary Alice jumped off the bike in front of the front door, rudely setting the bike down on the sidewalk. Her face took on a fixed, determined expression. Pushing the door open, she went in, searching for her dad. Country music blared over the loudspeakers. Finally she laid eyes on him, shooting pool with some guy on the other side of the room.

Mary Alice rushed over to the pool table. Her dad saw her right away. He gave her a big smile, but then his head snapped down, and his face became twisted. "Mary Alice, what are you doing here? You know minors aren't allowed in poolrooms. Are you trying to get me in trouble?

"I need to talk to you," she whined, her eyes red-rimmed from crying. "I need to talk to you in private."

Chuck Gallegon sighed deeply and placed his pool stick on the table. Facing the guy he was shooting pool with, Chuck said, "I gotta go talk to my daughter. Stay here, I'll be right back."

The guy, a big guy, began to get angry. "You got hold of my money," he growled. "You better get back here in a hurry to finish this game if you know what's good for you."

"Don't worry buddy," Chuck said, giving Mary Alice a little shove. "This won't take long."

They went out the front door so no one could listen to their conversation. "Now what do you want," Chuck said in a low, steady voice.

Mary Alice met her dad's eyes straight on. "Coach Mike needs to see you right away. "

"What! Can't this wait until tomorrow?"

"No dad, something important came up and he needs to talk to you tonight."

Chuck Gallegon rolled his eyes. "Well, I'll be a monkey's uncle. This seems awfully silly to me. Are you sure this can't wait?"

"No dad, this is really important."

"Well…" Chuck was thinking. He looked back inside, through a wide storefront window. The guy he was shooting pool with was waiting impatiently, stomping and peering in their direction.

"Okay, let's go" he told her. He steered her toward his pickup truck, parked in the back.

Mary Alice spun around. "I came here on a bike I borrowed. Help me put it…"

We'll come back to get it later," Chuck assured her. "Now get in the truck. We gotta get out of here in a hurry."

They drove away fast, the truck peeling out on the gravel parking lot, scattering stones in all directions. Mary Alice looked back through the rear cab window. She could see the big guy outside the poolroom, shaking a fist at them.

"Are you gonna be in trouble with that poolroom man?" she asked her dad softly.

Chuck blew air through his nose and snorted. "Nothing I can't handle," he said, chuckling. "Besides, I'm ahead on money for a change. It's a good feeling."

Mary Alice was silent the rest of the way to Jack Bumblebee's bungalow. She was worried about what would happen. Would Sam Ridge hurt her dad?

They parked in front of the house. "Dad," Mary Alice said, her voice dropping to a whisper, "before we go in, I…I…well, I love you."

Chuck patted her knee. "I love you too Kitten…" he started to tell her, but she was already out of the truck cab. He joined her at the front steps and impulsively reached out and gave her a hug. He felt her stiffen slightly, then her arms went around him and she hugged him tightly. "Let's go in and see what Coach Mike wants," he said. A sudden chill feeling hit his heart, and it seemed a cold hand was running its fingers up his back to the nape of his neck. He shivered and went inside the bungalow with his daughter.

Sam Ridge was waiting for them in the throne room, resplendently dressed in the lengthy gold trimmed gown of a sorcerer. His hair was different too, long down to his shoulders with dreadlocks. Two of the flying serpents were hovering over his head. Sadly, George and Todd were still bound to the wall. The repulsive Jack Bumblebee, smirking madly, was standing between them.

Chuck looked around the room, trying to figure out what was going on around him. "Mike," he said, fixing his gaze onto the strangely attired coach, "is… is that you?"

"Sam Ridge is my mortal name, but after tonight you will call me your lord and master."

"What's going on here…" but before Chuck could say another word, Sam Ridge raised a wand and Chuck was left mute and paralyzed. Mary Alice screamed and rushed toward her dad, stopping when she slammed against an invisible wall. She slid down to the floor with her arms outstretched. With a pleading look in her eyes, she looked to see if George or Todd could help. No chance.

"Mary Alice!" Sam Ridge called out. "My dear sweet Mary Alice. My accomplice. You see, I needed your help in my grand schemes."

Mary Alice stared at Sam with absolute hatred. She felt her cheeks burn.

"Now, now, don't look at me like that," Sam told her like he was her favorite uncle. "You see, I had to get you involved. That is why I made it so easy for you to find my living crystal, and why I let your little friend capture me in the cornfield. Foolish child, did you really think you could save your dad? I'm afraid your little journey to the underworld sealed his fate. I have tricked you to bring your father to me and now he is mine."

Burying her head in her arms, Mary Alice couldn't bear looking at the evil sorcerer anymore. She did notice the invisible wall had had gone away because she no longer could feel any pressure against the back of her hands.

"All I have to do his breathe in your dad's fear and I shall become an immortal god, ruler of the world!" Sam Ridge loudly proclaimed. "Ah, his fear smells so sweet."

Sam Ridge came up behind Chuck, grabbed him by the throat and lifted him off his feet. With one hand the sorcerer pushed Chuck's head down. Then he began to inhale deeply from the top of his head.

"Daddy...Daddy..." Mary Alice cried out. She ran to her dad as he began to collapse. Skidding, she landed at his feet. She clutched his legs tightly, not letting go, tears rolling down her cheeks.

"How did you get through the invisible wall," Sam said with a puzzled expression, and then he began to wail loudly. "The tears...the tears of a young girl, it's burning me!" he screamed. He fell back and wiped a hand on the bare skin at his sleeve. One of Mary Alice's tears had splashed there, and the skin began to melt. The tear splash spread and soon the skin on his entire body began to liquefy. He howled with mingled anger and pain as he turned into a living skeleton. The bones in his jaws were still moving, but sound was no longer coming out. Suddenly the skeleton changed to dust, and Tom Ridge crumpled into a pile of filth.

Jack Bumblebee hurried over to the grimy remains of the wicked sorcerer and got down on his knees. Looking up at Mary Alice, he shrieked, "Look at what you have you done to my master!" and as he touched the filthy stuff of what was left of Tom Ridge, he also turned into a living skeleton that dissolved into a foul muck. While all this was going on, the flying serpents flew around madly, squealing in agony before they exploded into fireballs, fluttering to the floor as tiny flakes of black ash.

Mary Alice felt a hand on her shoulder. Turning around quickly, she saw George standing behind her. Todd was there too; both boys were released from the chains. Chuck Gallegan was no longer immobile. He looked at the others like he was wondering how he got in this house in the first place.

"It's all over, Mary Alice," George told her soothingly. "Sam Ridge has been destroyed, and Jack Bumblebee too. We'll take their ashes to the furnace in Washington Hall and send them back to the underworld forever."

"Somebody is going to have to explain all this to me," Chuck said.

Mary Alice looked up. For the first time in a long while, she smiled. "I will, Dad. But right now, I just want you to hold me."

## CHAPTER EIGHTEEN

▼

This day had the makings of the best Thanksgiving ever. Mary Alice was riding her mom's old bike again, this time she was on her way to Washington Hall to see George one more time. George had asked her to come; said he was ready to move on to Heaven, and he would like to say goodbye.

The morning was crisp but sunny, perhaps the last really nice day before the winter's snow and cold come blasting in. Geese flying overhead in their V formation were making their honking noise. Mary Alice gave them a fond glance, admiring nature's natural beauty. Her skin got all tingling. How good it was to be alive! She had never felt this happy before, but she had another very good reason. Her mother had come home! She was there now, preparing Thanksgiving dinner, making the house smell warm and delicious. And more good news! Her dad had agreed to seek treatment for his gambling sickness. That was why her mom had returned, to give him another chance. They were a family again.

She couldn't wait to see George. They had been through so much together. But it had all been worth it. Her dad was safe. And Sam Ridge was gone forever.

George had explained everything to her. Yes, it was true; Sam Ridge had used them as pawns in his grand schemes. He had tricked them through Jack Bumblebee in believing Sam's living crystal had to be retrieved, but it was all a ruse to bring Mary Alice's dad to his lair, the beige bungalow. How Sam was destroyed was even more intriguing. Sam Ridge was brought down by love, or rather the tears of love. The grief Mary Alice felt for her father was out of genuine love, and the tears of a pure-hearted young girl are acid to those who are evil.

George also let her in a little secret. It was he who had gotten rid of the invisible wall that had separated her from her dad. He didn't have much strength in that house, but he had enough to use a little ghostly magic, playing a hunch that if Mary Alice could get close to Sam Ridge, she might have the chance to put a damper on his plans. But even he had no idea Mary Alice had the power to destroy the evil sorcerer.

Todd was another matter. He still wouldn't give her the time of day in front of the other kids, still was a victim of peer pressure to act like a tough guy. Well...things were a little different. Every now and then, Mary Alice noticed Todd would give her far fetching looks. Who knows? Maybe someday they can actually be friends.

The Notre Dame campus was nearly empty being that most of the students were home for the Thanksgiving holiday. Mary Alice rode her bike on the diagonal sidewalks, entering the main quad. Thoughts of the Fighting Irish football team entered her mind. The undefeated team was on the west coast, ready to play the Southern Cal Trojans, also undefeated, the winner claiming the right to play on New Year's Day for the national championship. She hoped Tony Rice would break away for a couple of touchdowns!

Bells were ringing from the nearby church as Mary Alice parked her bike in front of Washington Hall. The door was slightly ajar, so she went in. All was quiet inside, no trumpet sounds, thank you very much. But where was George? He told her to meet him here.

She turned to go up the balcony steps when she noticed fog was sliding in under the crack of an office door. The fog thickened as it rose, moving around the lobby a few moments before settling down on the floor. In an instant the fog took the shape of a young man in his twenties. It was George.

"Can't you ever enter a room like a normal person," Mary Alice said, grinning sheepishly.

"Well, good morning to you too," he muttered quietly. "You insist on forgetting I'm not a normal person. I'm a ghost."

"So here I am," Mary Alice said abruptly. "Why did you want to see me?"

"I want you to escort me to Heaven," George said simply.

Mary Alice swallowed hard. How could a living person take somebody to Heaven? She couldn't imagine it. What would Heaven look like? Would you see angels and harps and stuff like that? But she could see how important this was to George—for him this was a commitment for all eternity. And if Mary Alice were a good friend, she would do anything to help him get there. "George, how do we begin?" she asked.

"I'm not exactly certain."

"But you said – "

"I know what I said," he interrupted. "All I know is… I have to go through the tunnel of Notre Dame Stadium. Will you go with me?"

Mary Alice smiled. "You know I will." She opened the door, stepping aside to let George pass by.

"There must be something special about you, Mary Alice," George said. "Perhaps you can truly help me get to Heaven."

The tunnel, the main entry to Notre Dame Stadium, angles down to the playing field. Mary Alice and George stood at the bottom of the tunnel, looking out at the turf, and the rows and rows of empty wood plank seats.

"I really have no idea why we are here," George said somberly. Right after saying this, a wind began to blow in their faces, softly at first, but soon turning into a gale. Mary Alice and George had to close their eyes and bend into the wind to keep from being swept away. It didn't take long for the wind to die down. And when the ghost and the girl raised their heads, they couldn't believe what was going on before their eyes.

The playing field was crowded with football players, dozens of them, all fitted in the old-fashioned leather helmets and the skimpy shoulder pads worn by those in the old photos. Some were kicking footballs while others were throwing passes, and even others were practicing tackling. Directing all this was a stocky man, short in height and rather bald. He had on yellow football pants and a bulky blue sweatshirt. He also had a whistle in his mouth, but took it out when he swiveled to face George.

"Where have you been, Gipp," he barked. "We've got a game with Carnegie Tech Saturday, and we haven't beaten them in three years. Now get in here. We need all the practice we can get."

"Is that God?" Mary Alice asked George.

"No, that's the Rock," George said, laughing. "He just sometimes thinks he's God."

Off to the side, sitting on the hard wood seats near the end zone, were a man and a woman, and they were waving furiously. "That's my mom and dad," George said, waving back. "You know, they have never seen me play."

"Hurry it up, George," Rock told him. "We don't have much time."

George turned his head and looked straight at Mary Alice. His smile of friendship was like a warm fire on a dark cold night. He gave her a hug, and kissed her forehead. "Thanks for everything," he said, and he let her go and ran out to join the other players. Someone threw a football to him, and he dropped it to the ground and kicked it. The ball soured high in the clear blue sky. That was when the fierce wind came up again. Mary Alice had to bend over and close her eyes, just like before. When the wind calmed down, and she could look up again, the playing field was empty, and she was all by herself.

Hopping on her mom's rusty bicycle, she thought of George, how brave he is, how happy he must be, and she knew he was in Heaven.

"Take me home," she said to her mother's old bike.